T0267510

Everything Flirts

John Simmons Short Fiction Award

Everything Flirts

Philosophical Romances

Sharon Wahl

University of Iowa Press · Iowa City

University of Iowa Press, Iowa City 52242
Copyright © 2024 by Sharon Wahl
uipress.uiowa.edu
Printed in the United States of America

Cover design by TG Design
Text design and typesetting by Sara T. Sauers
Printed on acid-free paper

No part of this book may be reproduced or used in any form or by any means
without permission in writing from the publisher. All reasonable steps have
been taken to contact copyright holders of material used in this book. The
publisher would be pleased to make suitable arrangements with any whom it
has not been possible to reach.

This is a work of fiction. All of the characters, names, organizations, places,
and events portrayed are either products of the author's imagination or are
used fictitiously.

Epigraph page 38, from the *Autobiography of Bertrand Russell*: copyright of
the Bertrand Russell Peace Foundation and the publishers Taylor & Francis.
Epigraph page 38, from *A History of Western Philosophy*: copyright © 1945
Bertrand Russell; copyright renewed © 1972 Edith Russell; reprinted with the
permission of Touchstone, an imprint of Simon & Schuster L.L.C., all rights
reserved; electronic rights: copyright the Bertrand Russell Peace Foundation.
Epigraph page 50, reprinted with the kind permission of Rachel Aviv.
Epigraph page 128, from *Cybernetics,* second edition, page 133: copyright ©
1961 Massachusetts Institute of Technology, by permission of the MIT Press.

Library of Congress Cataloging-in-Publication Data
Names: Wahl, Sharon, 1956– author.
Title: Everything Flirts: Philosophical Romances / Sharon Wahl.
Description: Iowa City: University of Iowa Press, [2024] | Series: John
    Simmons Short Fiction Award | Includes bibliographical references.
Identifiers: LCCN 2024012669 (print) | LCCN 2024012670 (ebook) |
    ISBN 9781609389970 (paperback) | ISBN 9781609389987 (ebook)
Subjects: LCSH: Love—Psychological aspects. | Love—Philosophy.
Classification: LCC BF575.L8 W337 2024 (print) | LCC BF575.L8 (ebook) |
    DDC 152.4/1—dc23/eng/20240529
LC record available at https://lccn.loc.gov/2024012669
LC ebook record available at https://lccn.loc.gov/2024012670

In memory of my father, Orin A. Wahl

And for Jonathan

Contents

I am anxious to leave on record at least in this place my
deliberate opinion that any great improvement in human
life is not to be looked for as long as the animal instinct of
sex occupies the absurdly disproportionate place it does.

—DIARY OF JOHN STUART MILL

The more I became consumed by this passion, the less
I was able to indulge in philosophy.

—PETER ABELARD

Give me chastity and continence, but not yet.

—*Confessions* OF ST. AUGUSTINE

Zeno and the Distance Between Us

HOW WIDE IS THE arm of a seat in a dark theater? We are both touching the wooden armrest, leaning into it from either side with our bony elbows and our thin naked arms. Our shoulders are so close that the loose sleeves of our tee shirts almost touch. How different it would be if my arm could pass right through. But it is only this solid piece of wood between us that allows us to get so close. Inanimate things accept touch, but can't return it; so simple things get rubbed smooth. Look how this armrest has been battered with attention, polished and popcorn-oiled by all the hands that have sat here with nothing else to hold.

Emerging past the armrest, side by side on our blue-jean thighs, our flickering hands. We are blue in movie light, and the shadows of our finger joints, our knuckles, our bony wrists, are both spooky and exquisite. We could be statues. Marble in moonlight.

Have I ever touched him? Once, as I walked behind him at a crowded party. I put my hand on his shoulder, lightly, just barely resting my fingers on the fabric of his shirt. He was talking and didn't notice. I did this only once, though we were there all night. The room was dim, and always people dancing and chatting and bumping each other as they passed with drinks. And I, just passing, could easily have reached out again to steady myself with a light hand on his tee shirt, pressing just enough this time to test how thin his shoulder was or feel the muscles along his spine.

His index finger curls and straightens. Mine does the same, as if to know what he is feeling is to feel him. Even this tiny movement reminds my finger of my knee, the knee of the finger, returns the texture of the cloth between them.

How wide is the arm of a seat in a dark theater? The philosopher Zeno gave this paradox of motion: to reach him, I must cross half the distance between us. Then half the distance remaining; then half of that, and half again, and again, and again. I can only go halfway.

Proving, motion is impossible.

And yet.

That night at the party, for instance. He walked outside onto the porch, where it was quite dark, and looked up at the sky, maybe at the stars, recognizing a constellation, or maybe just in a vague way admiring the lights in so much dark. No one else was around. I had followed him at a little distance and stood leaning against the doorframe pretending to be part of the room inside, the music, the dancing and drinking. But I was there with the sky and the crickets, watching him. And for minutes he stood with his beer on the porch railing. His back to me. His bony shoulder. Perfectly natural, it would have been perfectly natural for me to walk up, reach a hand to his shoulder, the hand of, Hey don't want to startle you what's up, and leave it there, just friendly, the dark, the drink, the music. A warm night, starting to cool with a little breeze, but sweaty for dancing. Just out there for the breeze. Great party, isn't it? Perfectly natural for his arm to go around me, just loosely around my waist. And as we talked, friendly and hardly able to see each other in the dark, so it was hardly real, moving his hand lower to rub my hip. Tonight we ran into each other checking out movies from the library. We talked about an actress we both loved, who had a new movie. We both asked at the same time, Do you want to—? That was easy. Now, for two hours, his hand will be in reach. His leg is in reach. My hand is on my thigh, like his, and my thigh is so close to his that moving the hand from mine to his, fitting my long thin fingers between his longer ones, would take less effort than shaking hands.

But look at him. In the first minutes of this movie, a woman, the beautiful actress, has lost her husband and daughter in a car wreck. Look at his face, the worry in his eyes and brows, the way his lips, drawn together, seem bruised. Look how sad this movie has made him. Since the accident his fingers have tensed and dented his thigh. Now the actress is walking along a walled garden. She looks distracted and hollow. She trails her fingers along the brick wall as she walks, then with no warning rakes the bare flesh of her arm against the bricks until it bleeds. His fingers clutch into fists. He stares wide-eyed at the screen as tendrils of blood cross her arm.

His hand is still close to mine, really it's only five or six inches away. But covering a hand clenched into a fist would be a gesture of comfort, soothing him of some pain that perhaps I shared. And that isn't true. I'm dismayed. This movie is the wrong thing to be thinking about. When I touch him I want him to be aware of me as skin, to notice how the skin on the back of my hand is so tight it feels polished, while the palm is warmer, moister, plumper. If you take someone's hand in sympathy, you can't trace your fingers up and down his arm and give him goosebumps. You can't tease all his attention into the space between his first and second fingers.

As soon as his hand relaxes, I tell myself, I'll move my hand, and cover it. As soon as it comes back onto his thigh. I rub my palm on my cheek to test it: not damp and not dry, very soft. It smells just slightly of cucumber soap.

It seems so simple now. Once we were standing at the porch railing arm in arm, I could have said, so easily, Come on, let's look at the garden, let's see what the flowers do at night. And led him by the hand down the stairs, and stayed hand in hand as we told each other how good the roses and the lavender smelled, and wow, what was that? Along the fence, a vine that smells fantastic, oh, it's honeysuckle, isn't it? Isn't that what honeysuckle looks like? And we would finally drop hands, so that he could break off a tendril of honeysuckle and loop it behind my ear. And I would pick a couple sprigs of lavender for him, and pretend that it was difficult to attach them, as he had no buttonholes, though I would pretend there were and try to poke through the tee shirt, or through his collarbone where there should be a collar button, or through his nose that wasn't pierced after all, finally stuffing them into the front pocket of his shirt, crushing the little flowers to release more scent.

And here he is, just as close as in the garden. Instead of relaxing, his hands have left his thighs to grip each other's arm at the elbow, to clench and comfort each other. His legs are pressed together at the knees. His shoulders are hunched from slumping lower and lower in the seat. Only his eyes are still wide open, peering up at the screen in fascinated anticipation of the further pain he expects it to inflict.

I shift my elbow onto the armrest, so he won't be quite so far away. I edge the elbow slowly, deliberately across and over the armrest, for the first time violating his unpatrolled chair space. He is so skinny and so tightly huddled that it's still inches from the closest part of him. I watch him breathe, all locked up.

Watching him instead of the movie feels like stealing something. It is a little like watching someone sleep. We are in another world, and the expressions left behind on our faces are vulnerable. But why would I want to watch a movie, when he is here? It's such a luxury to look over and see him next to me. In my imagination his face always lacks detail. Here it is, all filled in. Here is his cheek shaved very smooth with an eyelash fallen onto it, and his nose without any bumps on it. Profiles take getting used to; they don't always look like the same face.

Especially this close. The nose is larger, and the mouth is smaller, and there's a different chin.

He is so still. Only his eyes move; he blinks. I could put my hand on his leg. His leg is right here. It's just a leg. I look at it and feel fond of the way his knee has rubbed the jeans into thready patches. His thigh would feel hard and solid, like mine. Harder, maybe. There's the familiar lump of keys in his right pocket, maybe tissues, stuff wadded up. Loose folds at the hips, such skinny hips.

All the time I've been watching him he hasn't once looked at me. It's a little insulting. At first I watched sideways, sneakily, but he didn't notice and now I'm just outright staring. I can't believe he doesn't see me. I imagine putting my hand on his thigh, wrapping my fingers into the inside of the thigh a little. What would he do? I imagine my hand sitting on his thigh, squeezing it, my poor excited finally happy hand, and him staying still and staring up at the screen and just blinking.

The movie is already half over.

The scent of honeysuckle was so strong, he said he could find me just by smelling. So I ran into the shadow of a tree and told him to close his eyes and try. No, I couldn't smell him in the dark under the tree, lavender is delicate. But that wasn't the point. There we were, giggling in the dark. With my eyes closed, I couldn't help but walk with arms stretched out, to take slow steps and grope the air. I heard him stepping on leaves, and he heard me, stepping and giggling, so of course we found each other, our stretched arms hit and withdrew from the species' monster instinct, Help, Something in the dark! Then reached again, is that a hand, yes, and what is this? Finding arms and pulling on them, finding a head and hair, textures and bumps, touching it as though it was a thing to be identified, a new thing we hadn't expected to find. Really it was a strange thing in the dark, all the parts of us seeming to be unconnected and needing to be put together—the scoops and hollows, thicks and thins—until finally they all fit, my hands on his back pulling his chest to my breasts, and even our belt buckles cooperatively clicking.

I look over to see if he is wearing a belt. He isn't. Neither am I.

Some months have passed in the movie, and the grieving woman has decided to take a lover. Finally. Of course I'm hoping that watching a love scene with a woman he finds attractive might remind this man in the seat next to me of other, less distant, possibilities. But as soon as they are alone the actress undresses and commands her admirer to strip. This is a man who has loved her secretly for many years. She gives him thirty seconds.

"No," the man next to me says. The word is forced out of him, in pain for the man this time.

"He should just leave," I say.

"Shhh," he says gently, as the woman onscreen is saying something else, something equally cruel, and he wouldn't want to miss it.

Under the tree, under his shirt, under my hands, his skinny back, wingtips, spine, his skinny ribs, ticklish if touched too lightly. Then we are kissing. A nuzzle of beard stubble, then his lips. The rest is easy. This is how it starts this time, the party and the porch, the flowers, the tree. I have a copy of the *Kama Sutra* illustrated with Indian miniatures. My favorite of them shows a man being driven by horse cart between his lovers: a plump woman with a parrot who sits astride his lap; a slender pale woman who lies underneath him in a garden; a dark playful one who squats on top of him under a tree full of squirrels and white herons. They've spread a gold carpet underneath the tree, and the woman, while raising and lowering herself on the naked man, pets a small deer. That is me in the horse cart, on my way to try again, and all of the women are him, each time in a different colored tee shirt, each setting a different missed seduction: on the walk home after we met in a bookstore; in his car, the night he drove me home from a party and I asked him to drop the others off first; in the theater, another dark, close, logical, suggestive place.

We always meet accidentally, and I'm always unprepared. Even when I'm hoping desperately to see him, hanging around the bookstore or a café because those are places he might appear—even then, I try to make the meeting look accidental. The lovers in the *Kama Sutra* would never let this happen. They would have spent the day being oiled and perfumed and painted, laying golden carpets under the trees, choosing incense and ragas for their powers of aphrodisia, instructing the servants as to when they might appear with wine or trays of perfect fruit. Their intentions couldn't possibly be mistaken, or the women themselves, resisted. I, however, have not painted the palms of my hands with henna, nor taken a bath perfumed with sandalwood. I'm wearing a tee shirt and jeans. Nothing that suggests it wants to be touched, the way silk or lace would give out instructions on their own.

I roll up the sleeves of my tee shirt. That isn't much, but there is so little I can do here. I wish I had a tattoo, something that could be revealed. I take off my shoes and my socks, and put my bare feet up on the seat in front of us. Look, something naked. Look at the toes, the high arches. The delicate anklebone.

His eyes never leave the screen. The movie is in French, which I don't understand, and I haven't been reading the subtitles, so by now I have no idea what is happening. The expressions that cross his face are completely incomprehensible.

I finally edge my elbow far enough across the armrest that it nudges his. All my attention is in this elbow, and it is feeling quite coquettish. It bumps him again, rubbing against him suggestively, Hey there, Mr. Elbow.

"Oh, sorry," he whispers, as though he is crowding me, as though he has accidentally jostled a complete stranger. He leans against the armrest on his other side.

I leave quietly, thinking he won't notice. He is quiet, too, so quiet I don't realize he's followed me until he catches me right outside the theater, on the sidewalk under the bright marquee.

"I was not in the mood for that," I say.

"Yeah, that was pretty intense," he says.

"Yup," I say. I sit down on the sidewalk to put on my socks and shoes, right down on the flat cement, deliberately ungraceful. This confuses him: Did I carry my shoes into the theater? Wasn't I wearing them? Where did they come from? Maybe he is seeing me for the first time.

He says it's hard to talk after something like that. He says he will walk me home. We leave the Loop for streets with the lights farther apart, with large trees shadowing the sidewalks, leaf-shaped shadows mixing with our leggy shadows that grow taller in one direction then shorter in the other between the streetlights, Look at that, and tree frogs, which hush when you get too close, he tells me, Listen, and crickets, which don't; the night still warm though it is late, and both of us are sleepy, and shy.

The true man wants two things: danger and play. For that reason he wants woman, as the most dangerous plaything.

—FRIEDRICH NIETZSCHE, *Thus Spoke Zarathustra*

I Also Dated Zarathustra

On the Dating Game

It's not the questions that count, and it's not exactly the answers. You ask a silly thing—"What kind of fruit would you be?"—and you hope a voice on the other side of the dividing panel, one from the row of three men on stools the audience can see but you cannot, will reach through the makeup and studio laughter to give a sign that he knows, yes, this is stupid, but what we want is not stupid: Who, after all, knows how to find the person he will love?

I had looked nearly everywhere else and decided that if necessary, and it seemed to be necessary, I would look here, too. I would sit in a tight short dress with my legs placed at an advantageous angle to the camera, crossed at the knees with one high heel dangling from my toes. It's a favorite pose, and successful. The men I was quizzing couldn't see it, but the cameraman was driven crazy. With each question I asked, he returned to dwell on the ankle and bare heel.

Well then. What kind of fruit *would* he be?

Bachelor Number One? "Something that will make a really great pie. And that's a promise. I am one dependable fruit."

Bachelor Number Two? "I'd be figs, two fat brown figs. And I'm always ripe."

Bachelor Number Three? "I am a north wind to ripe figs. I am a prophet of the lightning and a heavy drop from the clouds. I am an intoxicated sweet lyre—a midnight lyre, a croaking bell which no one understands but which still must speak!"

I didn't move but I was suddenly aware of my thighs, of the insides of my arms. Bachelor Number Three had a voice like a cloud speaking, traces of roar and thunder and waves held together with honey-cello. But what did I know about him? He might be ridiculous, a resonantly rambling fool. But when a man is mysterious enough, when I have no idea which things will be good or bad or where the problems will be or even what will happen next, it makes me think that anything might be possible.

"Num Ber Two! Num Ber Two!" the audience chanted during the thinking music.

Number One hugged and kissed me. Number Two slipped a note with the number of his hotel room down the front of my dress. Number Three stiffly bowed.

He was older than the others. His eyebrows were shaggy and his mustache needed trimming. He wore a long black coat, which would never, in the course of our acquaintance, be removed.

He bowed and shook my hand. Then, lifting his eyebrows, he peered at it: a hand, yes, in his hand, a hand attached to other parts of a fairly beautiful woman with whom he was about to spend a weekend in Las Vegas. That's where they were sending us, to the glittering neon desert, to try our luck.

"Ah," he said. "What a long and beautiful hand! It is the hand of one who has always distributed blessings. But now it holds fast him you seek, me, Zarathustra."

On Love of the Strange, and of Men

Oh, it's a love of aching things, not sweet things, a love of stars, long silences, birds that sing at night. A love like an old Victorian house that is almost empty: a winding staircase to a room paneled in dark wood, its worn polish dimly reflecting light from a chandelier with yellow bulbs, a few notes of Chopin played in another wing of the house by an overnight guest who does not speak. (I would love him, too, thin like a carved rail of the staircase, awkwardly holding a glass of wine at dinner so that you might think his hands hadn't comfortably mastered the world; and yet, the Chopin.) A love like stamps from a country whose name you don't recognize, exquisite writing in a script you can't read or a language you don't know.

I have never loved anything I've understood.

"All mousetraps of the heart have now again been set! And wherever I raise a curtain, a little night-moth comes fluttering out." I was on the balcony, standing in the hot sun looking out over the Nevada desert, where the bare mountains were made beautiful by shadows. Zarathustra, in the hotel room, stretched his hands to the blasting air conditioner and spoke to himself.

The strange are often the best defended; that is how they have kept themselves strange. "I am not on my guard against deceivers, I must be without caution," Zarathustra said. Their hearts are not guarded deliberately, but by being essentially impenetrable.

It's a love that is like loneliness.

Of Balancing on Four Legs

It was a warm night, with lots of neon. It was one of those nights when the world seemed to be made not of people, but of couples. Everywhere I looked bodies were paired together, connected at the hands or more tightly around the waist, awkward animals walking with a tilt and lean, off-balance, unsymmetrical. They reminded me of those children's books with the pages cut in three, each section the top, middle, or bottom of an animal, so that the normal old heads and legs and bellies could be made into sillier creatures: a salamousowl, a girelephish, a pandazebrogator.

And yes, I wanted to be part of it all. Oh, to be damply interlaced at the palms. To be affectionately leashed, tethered in the crowded streets, appended. To make a wider obstacle on the sidewalk, a wandering self-absorption that others had to navigate, rather than this narrow thing that darts and slips politely by.

But Zarathustra understood nothing of this. He would walk between or duck under the arms of people clearly together, something I by instinct could not do. It was impossible to truly accompany him, to predict and accommodate his walking speeds or stopping places. He seemed to resent being tied down, even by gravity. He walked with high fast steps and frequently bumped into things. Really he couldn't see very well; until he was at arm's length he wasn't completely certain what he was looking at. This meant that everything out of reach was immensely interesting, and the things close by merely obstacles.

And so we wandered, over the Brooklyn Bridge, into the great pyramid. When he pushed people aside to get a better view of the volcano or the pirates, I apologized and petted them, winked and shrugged: He's hopeless, what can I do? And really most people didn't mind so much once they looked at him. He was so completely taken over by the spectacle, so silly looking and so utterly happy, that often enough they ended up watching us instead.

If there were a Couple Game, a prize for the oddest match on the Vegas Strip, we would have won. Zarathustra could have been my father. Or crazy. Perhaps he was extremely wealthy? Something the casinos had flown in. No doubt I was being paid well. Madmen don't get girls with legs this long. The casino had hired me, to raise the stakes. Or he had hired me, for much the same function. Oh wasn't he a lucky man!

We just didn't look like we were on a date. I wondered if this was why the show had assigned us a chaperone—to give Zarathustra a backup option, and to let me off the hook. Surely this odd man couldn't be my type?

"Perhaps you would like a game of poker?" the chaperone had suggested, after dinner.

"I have played dice with the gods at their table, the earth," said Zarathustra.

"Oh, really? And where was this?"

The chaperone was a motherly type. She was a mother-in-law on a honeymoon who wanted desperately to be a fairy godmother. We had tickets to a show, coupons for free drinks, a hundred dollars in betting tokens, all of which she had bestowed upon Zarathustra, all of which had entered the pockets of his coat, never to be seen again.

She had tried to take the coat from him back in the hotel room. It was thick black wool, buttoned from his chest to his knees, and must have felt like wearing a portable oven. Still, it seemed possible that he had simply forgotten it was there. The chaperone suggested, coquettishly reaching for the top button, that she would make him more comfortable. Zarathustra said to her, "This is the tarantula's cave! Do you want to see the tarantula itself?" She didn't. She never mentioned it again.

I had said nothing. By then I'd come to enjoy the prospect of removing the coat myself at the end of the night. I pictured my long arms snaking from behind, my bare skin on his black wool, undoing him button by button.

And what was Zarathustra thinking, when he looked at me? Did he like tall redheads? Did he wish I was wearing more? "You have the most lovely shoulders," as the chaperone put it, winking at Zarathustra, who missed his cue for a courtly compliment.

It was difficult to imagine either of them on a date. She needed to have always been married; he needed to be taken by the arm and gently steered, directed this way or that with no mention made of the change of pilot. Or so I had thought; that was an innocent time, early evening.

"Try your luck!" the chaperone said, giving each of us a quarter as we passed a row of slot machines. They jingled and blinked happily among themselves like well-fed babies in need of occasional burping.

Zarathustra fed the nearest one his quarter, and I dropped mine in after, doubling the bet. The dizzy smile started up, spinning to lock on cherry, cherry, cherry. Quarters poured out. It was a good sign, I thought.

Zarathustra picked up a quarter and gave it back to the chaperone, then walked on. The chaperone had a wordless fit. She saw that yes, we really did intend to walk away. This was her chance. A thousand quarters: she looked hungrily at the pile, thinking that among so many there must be others that would win, she had only to find them, to kiss each frog and find the princes.

And so we left her. We didn't need a chaperone; we had his coat.

We walked for hours. The signs, the palm trees, the cars, the casinos, the people he passed on the street and the things they carried, all seemed to Zarathustra equally there for entertainment. The boy whose cotton candy he sampled (gazing in rapture at the pink cloud, plucking a wisp from it, licking tentatively at the barely there) had no right to scream at him, no, not when one possessed an object so delicious! Not when one possessed an object he wanted. I wasn't able to explain this to the boy or his father, but bought the boy another cone and a small teddy bear, hoping he wouldn't notice how much it resembled Zarathustra.

When I caught up with him again, a uniformed chauffeur had handed Zarathustra a vividly illustrated brochure of a desert brothel and was offering to drive him there. Zarathustra seemed confused that the pamphleteer was not, as he had naturally (so he insisted) assumed, a philosopher or revolutionary. Clearly anyone distributing printed material deserved his full attention.

"Ah," he said, standing in a bright spotlight to study the pamphlet. As he considered the transcendent ideologies of Daisy and Trixie, his shadow roamed over the side of a building across the street. He raised his arms and the shadow tried to climb through the window of a hotel room much too small for it. Two blonde teenaged girls approached and the arms went after them, straining for a squeeze, wiggling fingertips poked their knees and tried to trip them, the pamphlet waved madly over their bodies as they escaped unclutched. The shadow shrugged. Zarathustra shook his head at it disapprovingly. "I must keep it under stricter control—otherwise it will ruin my reputation."

I pulled him away by the arm, and found a moth hole in his coat sleeve, which fit my little finger like a ring. Z didn't seem to notice, so I kept it there. By this time it was becoming quite clear how much he needed me.

Of Dancing Things

"Listen," said Zarathustra. "It is night: now do all leaping fountains speak louder." We were sitting side by side on the low concrete ledge of the fountains in front of our hotel.

"And what do they say?"

"They are deep but without thoughts, like little secrets, like after-dinner nuts."

Zarathustra had his hand in the shallow water, plucking it with his finger, a soft plink-plink, plink-plink.

I slipped off my shoes and stepped in. My legs were a lovely blue in the reflected light. The pool was ankle deep, gently swirled and bubbled by the water spraying and tumbling in the middle.

Zarathustra scooped some pennies from the bottom of the pool, a few of the good luck pennies that were everywhere, and dropped them in again. They plopped straight back to the bottom, shy as frogs.

I made a wish, then threw in another penny. "I know what the water says. It says it's given up waiting for the pennies to swim. It wants people to throw goldfish, instead."

"Everything is asleep," Zarathustra said. "Even the water is asleep. Its eye looks at me drowsily and strangely. But it breathes; I feel it. And it is dreaming, look how it tosses and turns."

The air was warm, the water was warm. My feet were delighted. I walked through the shallow pool to the other side of the fountains on my blue legs, nudging pennies with my toes. Which felt better, stork steps, or fish steps? Which felt better, going from the air to the water, or the water to the air?

Zarathustra couldn't see it, but I was dancing. The water's hands slipped teasing through my fingers. My tall partners, the palms, swayed out of reach above me. The desert breezes came in now and then, stretched across us like a chorus line. Each of us with our private shivers.

I thought it would be nice, on a night like this, to fly. I left the water in a balletic leap, toes neatly pointed, one arm up, one to the side. But when I came down, I slipped on the pennies. I slid into a sharp pain—a bottle cap. My foot was cut. Zarathustra, in his brown leather boots and thick coat, came striding through the water to see what I was swearing at.

The cut wasn't deep; a small bleeding gouge on the side of my big toe. I dried it with tissue, and found a bandage in my purse. But Zarathustra was at war: there were to be no bottle caps among the pennies. He went down on hands and knees to search them out. His coat settled into the water reluctantly, floating and full of pocketed air, then sponging and swelling and sinking.

At first he was amusing, almost gallant. The eradication of sharp edges, the world made safer for toes. But he went on and on, crawling through the water, attacking nickels then releasing them, puzzling over gum wrappers and bits of palm leaf, banishing all manner of suspicious things to his wet pockets.

I wanted to go. I wanted a drink, and I said so. I wanted a cold, numbing, double margarita. Zarathustra ignored me, or maybe didn't hear. I said this louder. Putting on my shoes made my toe hurt more. "Come on," I said. Zarathustra tucked another bottle cap into his coat pocket. Probably they were falling back out again as he crawled. "This is ridiculous!" I shouted.

"All fish talk like that; what they cannot fathom is unfathomable," he said.

"I'm going inside," I said. At the hotel entrance I turned back to see if he had followed. He hadn't. He lay in the fountain stretched full length, legs spread, arms wide, his hands flapping and spanking the water, cooling his overheated addled brain and burbling.

On the Compassion of the White Tigers

Sometimes it helps to be drunk. One stiff margarita and I remembered how much I liked being wet, how charming I would look with my hair thoroughly soaked and shaken into ringlets. The fountain would tell me so itself, really, I was ready to hear all sorts of things. I was ready to sing along.

But Zarathustra had finished his bath. I found him wandering the main corridor of the hotel, waving his arms and spraying drops like a happy, wet dog.

I preceded him at a safe custodial distance. He didn't notice me; being human was sufficient camouflage.

The corridor led past a large white room, the mountain-kingdom throne room of the resort's white tigers, and there Zarathustra came to a sudden, astounded stop. Two white tigers lay on the floor not far from him, gazing into a distance we were certainly no part of.

"Ah, my brothers! If only my lioness Wisdom had learned to roar fondly!"

He sat down on the floor of the marble walkway and spoke to them, earnestly and at great length.

Their heads went slowly side to side, looking at everything as though they already knew it in their painted kingdom of empty white spaces and artificial things, snow in their minds. They had beautiful intelligent expressions and seemed complete, resigned to a stable satisfaction, not requiring further enlightenment.

He told them everything. I leaned half behind a marble pillar and listened.

"I have always wanted to caress every monster. A touch of warm breath, a little soft fur on its paw—and at once I have been ready to love and entice it. Love is the danger for the most solitary man, love of any thing *if only it is alive!*"

With my eyes closed, without the dreadful evidence of the wet coat, without the spreading streams of water the other casino-goers were gingerly stepping around as they passed him, looking at him and also trying not to look, not to spoil the night's glitter, not to wet their shoes, but especially not to hear him, surely this was gibberish, a language they didn't share, an animal speaking to animals, they pretended he was grunting—

With my eyes closed there were only his words, his words like little spotted night moths, and his deep voice. The most enticing sort of monster is a soul aching with ferocious tenderness.

"To be sure, I am a forest and a night of dark trees: but he who is not afraid of my darkness will find rose bowers too under my cypresses."

Did I think I could change him? Yes. Did I care what the others thought, the tip-toers, the avoiders of puddles? No. Did I think he would escort me through the dark cypresses into his rose bower? Yes. I pictured pale yellow climbing roses, a weathered bench strewn with fallen petals. I thought he had made the bower with its little bench so that I would have a place to sit.

"Ah, my friends, it is the evening that questions thus within me. Forgive me my sadness! We were made for one another, you gentle, strange marvels. And we have already learned so much with one another!"

He left them, much cheered and quieted, though still dripping, and followed me into the nearest bar.

On Learning to Drink from All Glasses

Zarathustra was fascinated by the little red straw that came with his margarita. It made slurps in such a nice assortment, hollow air sucks, loud bubble-burbles, liquid squishes. It suffered lime-pulp obstructions, it poked under cubes of ice, it vacuumed the last stray drops. He kept the straw in place between his lips and sipped liked a bird, lowering his head to the glass, tilting side to side, poking and hunting.

Finally the ice was sucked tasteless. But Zarathustra hadn't had nearly enough of the straw. Here and there on the empty tables were glasses left behind, some with enough color to be more than ice melt. *Come to us,* they called, *we are diluting.* The straw perked like a lower appendage. He couldn't resist. "He who does not want to die of thirst among men must learn to drink from all glasses," he said as he left me.

But most of these abandoned drinks were only drowned remains, melted ice and cherry stems and gnawed wedges of orange or pineapple. They were insufficiently alcoholic. He saw a fresh cocktail with a pink umbrella on another table, and with his straw, went directly to it. The woman who ordered the drink was horrified. She stared at the glass as though a man had popped out of it, not into it. It might happen again: acrobats could leap from the glass and stick their daiquiri-flavored tongues into her open mouth.

The couple at the next table said that someone really ought to call security. So I told them, leaning over confidentially, that Zarathustra was a paid comedian. "Yes, it's part of his act," I said. And truly, this was a stroke of genius.

"Oh!" they said, of course, it all made sense, and then they excitedly told the next couple. The world is so much nicer when it's making sense. I could see the rumor navigate the bar, who had heard and who hadn't, by the shift from flinches to smiles, then even to competition for Zarathustra's attention. Men called him over to shock their wives, a giggly, safely titillating little shock, and women offered up their drinks to him as he passed.

Zarathustra was delighted. Here was the world as he had intended it to be, here he was understood! Drunk, he was the perfect entertainer, a cross between a host and a clown, offering toasts and renaming all the drinks. "The Death of God!" he pronounced. "The Will to Power! Live Dangerously!"

The names were a bit mystifying to the drinking folk, but they loved him. He leaned over to suck another drink and lost his balance in a plump, elderly lap. The plump woman laughed and tried to grab him. "O Earth, you have grown too round for me!" he cursed.

"Live Dangerously!" they toasted. And to me, "He's good, isn't he? It's very clever."

Finally he came back to our table. He was merry and elated and fidgety, reaching out when fresh drinks passed, glazing over with alcohol and exhaustion. It was getting late. I was ready for a little gratitude. I moved my chair around the table very close to his. He still had the perky little straw in his mouth.

"You haven't yet tasted me," I said, and sucked on the end of his straw. It pinched his tongue, and he spat it out.

"Oh, your straw!" I said. It had fallen to the floor on the other side of his chair. I leaned over to get it, full across his lap, and while I was there I took the time to undo the two lower buttons of his cool damp wool cocoon. He was absolutely still. Inside and out. But he thanked me for the straw.

"Zarathustra," I said, sort of snuggling up to him but distracting him by pointing to a young couple kissing vigorously in a dark corner of the bar. "Look. What are they doing?"

"They are discovering new words."

"You mean, speaking with different tongues?"

"Before long they will be devising festivals!"

"I like it when they smile between kisses."

"Like cats they arch their backs, they purr."

"Well, look where his paw is . . ."

"You must not want to see everything."

"But I do. I think I do want to see everything, don't you?"

"For that you must have long legs."

"Let's see." I hooked my foot under his and stretched our legs out to measure them side by side. "Mine are longer! I thought so."

"You are making this cave sultry and poisonous, you evil sorcerer!"

"Sorcerer!"

"If I may tickle you with this name."

"I would prefer fingers."

Someone had left a marble in the ashtray on our table, a milky blue color, which Zarathustra began to roll across the table. I said it was the moon's right eye, sent to spy on us.

"He is lustful and jealous, the monk in the moon," Zarathustra said. "And what about you?"

"I am invulnerable only in my heels."

"Are you lustful? Do you like the girl over there, kissing?"

"One should speak about women only to men."

"Why? Tell me! What do you think of women?"

"They know how to blow horns and to go around at night and awaken old things that have long been asleep."

"Zarathustra," I said, "what are you hiding under your coat?"

"It is a little truth that I carry. But it is as unruly as a little child, and if I do not stop its mouth it will cry too loudly."

"Ah," I said. "Oh."

"You want to call it by a name and caress it. You want to pull its ears and amuse yourself with it."

"Yes," I said, "you're right, I do." I suggested that it was time to go back to the room.

Of an Introduction to the Ideal Woman

I led our trek from bar to bedroom through a small dense jungle, under waterfalls, over a green and gold wooden elephant, through beaded curtains into a dim red room painted with a harem scene. We leaned against the wall of bare-breasted dark-eyed women and pretended to choose a favorite, whispering to each other in the opium light, bumping and brushing hands in the purple shadows.

And then I found the perfect finale. On a pedestal advertising the week's performers was a classic chorus-girl mannequin, leg kicked high, arms wide. What a fetching pose, I thought. I could do that, too. A private Vegas floor show for Zarathustra.

I climbed up and danced a cancan with her, kicking my equally long legs, my arm across her shoulders. She was so cute. She was terribly sweet and happy. And Zarathustra gave us just the look I wanted, he gazed adoringly, ecstatically at the two of us intertwined. He said exactly what I wanted him to say: "Something unquenched, unquenchable, is in me, that wants to speak out. A craving for love is in me . . ." Oh yes, finally, yes yes yes. I let her go, and he walked up and reached out his arms and took her face in his hands, and kissed her.

He kissed her again, on her nose and her cheeks, her chin, on the corners of her smiling lips. He kissed her very nicely, too, sweet lingering little pecks. "Who could behold her smile and not dissolve into tears?" he asked me. Ah, yes. Indeed. Tears.

Then he stepped back to admire her, to take in the full measure of his luck. That this, this, should be waiting here, just for him.

She had those long showgirl legs (well, so do I), enhanced breasts (mine are real) set off by feather boas, and she had big unblinking blue eyes that said you were just exactly what she had all her life been waiting for (mine blink). Furthermore, you knew immediately that she would always look at you that way. In fact I think it's safe to say that most of one's first impressions of her were entirely accurate. Her behavior was in no way misleading. She might disappoint you, but she would never let you down. She was impeccably calm. Here was a woman who could face life's batterings and joys with the same unwavering expression: *Oh, how big and strong you are! J'adore!* She would never complain. She was patient and always willing to listen, but never intrusive. She was never jealous.

Now, I have softer breasts and better legs, and I am warm, I bend and squish and lick and sing, my mouth opens, my hands grip and stroke, I can dance a tango in spike heels. But I couldn't compete.

Zarathustra whispered to her, something I couldn't hear, then looked into her eyes as if she had agreed, yes, between them there was perfect understanding. Well, perhaps there was. I am only jealous of perfection when I see it taking a man away from me.

"I will rescue you from all corners," he said, gently pushing down her kicking leg. "I will brush dust, spiders, and twilight away from you."

He hoisted her from the platform, knocked over everything, and dislodged most of her feathers. After some fidgeting they fitted together with her stiff welcoming arms hooked over his left shoulder. He grasped her by her sequined ass and carried her toward the exit sign. She smiled at me over his shoulder, apparently delighted, as she was with all things. She went with him into the night with her eyes wide open.

"Come, cold and stiff companion! Let me show you my nocturnal world and the big, round moon and the silver waterfalls by my cave. The dog howls, the moon is shining. Here are caves and thickets: we shall go astray! Give me your hand! Or just a finger! Where now do you take me, you unruly paragon?"

I never saw him again. Though I still hear his voice from time to time, at night, when the ocean mutters to itself. Perhaps this was to be expected from a man who spent ten years in a cave, whose best friends were a serpent and an eagle. What other things could reach him on his mountaintop? Even the serpent had to be flown there in the talons of the eagle.

Perhaps if I had grown wings and thick talons, Zarathustra would have let me carry him away.

And Zarathustra ran and ran and found no one else and was alone and found himself again and again and enjoyed and relished his solitude and thought of good things, for hours on end.

—FRIEDRICH NIETZSCHE, *Thus Spoke Zarathustra*

6.21   *A proposition of mathematics does not express a thought.*

6.211   *Indeed in real life a mathematical proposition is never what we want.*

—LUDWIG WITTGENSTEIN, *Tractatus Logico-Philosophicus*

Tractatus Logico-Eroticus

1	*The world is all that is the case.*
1.1	*The world is the totality of facts, not of things.*
1.2	At colloquium dinner a month ago I sat across the long table from you. It was the first time I had seen you outside of class. There were flames between us, three candles. Your face was an apparition perfected by flame-flicker, distance, and a little wine.
1.201	Your face flickered as though I had projected it.
1.21	In the near-darkness I saw shapes I hadn't seen before: hollows in your cheeks and throat, dimples, the cleft in your chin. Shadow catchers. The contours of you.
1.3	I couldn't hear the conversation at your table end, only your laugh and isolated words that filled gaps in the speech of others between us. Your voice was distinguishable by a bounce in the vowels and a ring in the consonants. Irish, ironed at Oxford.

1.31   You sat compactly in the chair, upright or slightly forward, alert; you did not lean back. Your arms did not stray far. When you smiled, your lips did not let go of each other.

1.4   These facts that make up our outward selves, gestures seen from a distance by any stranger, words overheard in a context we did not make (dim light, or loneliness)—these facts that are most objective, we are unaware of; but they are what will suddenly cause another person to love us.

2   *What is the case—a fact—is the existence of states of affairs.*

2.011   *It is essential to things that they should be possible constituents of states of affairs.*

2.0121   *If things can occur in states of affairs, this possibility must be in them from the beginning.*

2.02   The first day of class, as you were leaving for campus, you dropped a large box of packing peanuts that you were carrying down the stairs of your apartment building. The box opened as it fell, spewing many times its volume of peanuts, snowdrifts and landslides to hear you tell it. The box tumbled one flight and landed solidly, but the peanuts floated, over the banister, up stairs, down halls, out the front door, onto the ledge of the second-floor window, which was just beyond your reach, even leaping.

2.021   You picked them all up, though it made you twenty minutes late for the first meeting of our seminar.

2.0211   The tyranny of time versus the catastrophe of disorder: duty versus aesthetics: one cannot leave packing peanuts in one's wake.

2.0212   I picture you thinking: Time ought to pause. That would be the proper thing, for time to wait politely until the dropping was undone, an accommodation for its not allowing things to be undone by going back and getting them right on another try.

2.022 As we waited in the seminar room, we discussed regulations concerning the lateness of professors, which none of the graduate students quite knew: Was it half an hour for professors with tenure, a quarter hour for those without?

2.023 I loved the airy fidgets of your fingers describing Styrofoam peanuts—your hands were impatient with weightlessness, with things lighter than the air disturbed as one approached to capture them. I loved your confidence that the outcome of this moral choice—us, or the peanuts—was self-evident. I loved the flakes of Styrofoam static-clung to the back of your sweater, precariously quivering at the vigorous motions of your chalk on the blackboard.

2.0272 *The configuration of objects produces states of affairs.*

2.1 In class, you seemed most comfortable looking at the person farthest from you. So that was the seat I chose. In class I was permitted, even expected, to watch you the entire time.

2.2 When we began our study of Wittgenstein's *Tractatus*, you said you had seen it for the first time in a bookstore when you were only fifteen. The strangeness of its form sent shivers down your spine: its look on the page, the orderliness of the numbers, the spareness and prophetic authority of its sentences. German and English stared across the pages seeming to translate each other, but also seeming to need yet another translation before you could know what was *meant*.

2.21 You bought the book, knowing nothing more about it. You said you were convinced it held mystical secrets, and read it like an apprentice combing a master alchemist's journal for experiments the master pursued late into the night without him, the deeper mysteries that did not permit a young and ignorant witness.

2.211   "But when I was fifteen, I also saw ghosts and had telepathy," you said. "I wanted everything to be more than it is."

2.212   I was jealous of everyone who heard you say this. They would all love you, they must. And of the slim red book you held, that you spoke to so fondly, and of my dead rival who made you shiver, Mr. Wittgenstein.

2.3   Frequently, while you met with other students in office hours, I was outside the cracked door pretending to wait for you.

2.301   I didn't think of listening at your door as eavesdropping. It was more like attending a rehearsal, sitting in the back of the auditorium while Horowitz practiced.

2.31   "Oh well," an undergraduate too easily, too cheerily excused her late paper, "things happen." "No, Susan," you replied sternly. "*Shit* happens. *Things* fall apart." A certain weariness in your voice implied a regret, even as you spoke, that the remark would be wasted on her.

2.32   As I heard the rustle of gathering up from inside, I would look anxiously at my watch, shaking my head, and walk off quickly toward another appointment for which I was, apparently, already late.

3   *A logical picture of facts is a thought.*

3.001   *'A state of affairs is thinkable': what this means is that we can picture it to ourselves.*

3.01   I had assumed, at the beginning, that nothing more would be possible. I had always given others this advice, in full confidence. Such things were not even. . . .

3.011 Consider the language in which I had expressed my objections: professor, student, authority, evaluation. But you are none of these categories. You are an airy thing, a small thing, a tight thing, a quick thing, a thing in a building with a light on at 4 a.m., predictable and then unpredictable, speaking and then silent, stopping to think with your lips just slightly parted, taking questions like a hungry chipmunk that must take a peanut from a boy's hand, approaching shyly then scurrying off with the nut to a safe distance, eating rapidly, and coming back, not as shyly, for more.

3.1 *In a proposition a thought finds an expression that can be perceived by the senses.*

3.11 One day I passed you in the hall deep in discussion with a visiting speaker. He asked where he might find a cup of coffee. You suggested the student center café, and said you would take him there.

3.12 I went to your office; the door was unlocked. The sweater you had worn in class that day was lying over the back of your chair. It was very soft, not like wool but like fur, a dark maroon with buttons down the front. I put my hand through the sleeve and stroked it and kissed it. I kissed the ribbed neck, then the front, each hard little button, outside and inside, filling the sweater with a mass of kisses like soap bubbles that would pop and disappear when touched, leaving a film of kisses where your body would be.

3.2 Your friend Mr. Wittgenstein said, in another place: "A philosophical problem has the form: 'I don't know my way about.'" Where in this did I get lost?

3.3 Last night I lay awake in bed imagining that I had cooked dinner for you. We ate and drank wine, and then we argued:

I was jealous of another student that you, that everyone, thought beautiful. It was a pointless argument, but I persisted, questioning you on the nature of thinking someone beautiful, was attraction necessarily involved, circling all the things I was afraid of, until finally you were so angry that you hit the table and a wine glass toppled and broke. Then you were gone. The imagination ended, but my pulse stayed hard and fast. It was our argument that caused this, your anger that I still experienced an hour later as I lay awake with my eyes open, even knowing that you knew nothing of this, you didn't scream at me or break the glass—

3.31   I still know what has happened, and what has not yet happened. I can remind myself. But my experience of merely possible events has taken on the greater intensity.

4.023   *A proposition must restrict reality to two alternatives: yes or no.*

4.031   *In a proposition a situation is, as it were, constructed by way of experiment.*

4.1   After colloquium dinner last week it was suggested that we all go to a movie. Some of us said yes, some said no, most said maybe; we would meet at a theater downtown in half an hour.

4.2   I arrived at the theater first, exactly on time. You were ten minutes late. We chatted cheerfully and easily in the presence of the others' expected arrival. The longer we waited, the less we said.

4.21   When the movie was about to start you suggested we give up and leave; the others weren't coming. I asked if you wanted to see the movie. You said yes. We laughed about this, but stood outside waiting, even after the film had begun.

4.3 Late in the movie, we leaned into each other, not in one motion but slowly, at first imperceptibly, until finally our shoulders met and lightly pressed. Through the fabric of my shirt I felt a gentle, growing warmth. We leaned through the credits, until the pointing finger of the house lights intruded. When we moved apart, that spot was still warm. All the blood in my body had rushed there, to pass through and spread that closeness to you everywhere inside me.

5.135 *There is no possible way of making an inference from the existence of one situation to the existence of another, entirely different situation.*

5.1361 *We* cannot *infer the events of the future from those of the present.*

5.2 Touch can be accidental. You may not have felt me, you may have noticed only the movie. Or maybe you felt my arm but stayed as you were because you were comfortable. Maybe you pretended the arm belonged to someone else, to an actress in the movie, or to a man you saw once in the supermarket and wanted but didn't dare to approach.

5.21 You may simply have been cold. But you were not shivering.

5.3 In fact the way we sat, each of us huddled against our shared armrest, leaving inches of empty seat on the opposite side, made the people on either side of us seem much farther than inches away. It seemed as though those people were not present at all: they were not with us. We were with each other.

5.4 After the movie, I walked to my car. You walked to your car. We both drove off. In my apartment I paced as though something was on its way, propelled by the energy of my steps. I went outside, to take longer steps.

5.41   I walked the two miles to campus. It was cloudy and a wind
came up; it started to rain. Your office window was dark. That
dark window made the campus completely empty.

5.5   It was five days until the next class. I waited with Tuesday's
class so much in my mind that days before, it already seemed
a solid place—you at one end of the oval table, the book-lined
walls of the seminar room behind you, the shelves of books
so familiar to me from years of browsing that I could see each
title on the spine, and I could see inside the books as well, the
frontispiece, random pages, so that the scene took on a surreal,
a portentous clarity.

5.51   Tuesday came. We entered the room, and left it again, two
hours later.

5.6   That you might feel as I do, seems to me impossible. That
you might not, is unthinkable: because that world would not
be the same as this one. And so I have decided, I must proceed
as though this is not merely thinkable, but possible. But what
can I do?

5.61   Just as there are no love potions, there are no love arguments: there are no deductions from which love follows as a
necessary conclusion.

5.62   And yet, the feeling in me believes that if it tells you enough,
it will pass itself on to you. No matter that we know differently,
even that saying what you feel is not possible. It has come to
believe that these are not just words but word-feelings, not an
account of the facts of my feelings but particles lightly fixed to
this page, floating things light as dust that might encounter
you directly.

5.631   *If I wrote a book called* The World as I found it, *I should have
to include a report on my body, and should have to say which
parts were subordinate to my will, and which were not.* . . .

6   *This is the general form of a proposition.*

6.01   What do you think about when you drive home at night, and the moon is rising, the late gibbous moon rising up through trees that only just dropped their leaves, so you can still smell them, a brown, crackly smell, and hear their dry crunch under the tires; what do you think of, then?

6.02   Some unnoticed number of hours ago the moon rose, just as I said, orange and a little off balance. Now and then small clouds pass it in the sky and make the trees disappear; only with the moon behind them can I see the branches.

6.021   As the moon gets higher it watches the progress of these pages. They were written by candlelight, as they are delicate. Your life must have secrets. Doesn't it? Yes, it must.

6.1   The entrance to my apartment is through a covered porch. On the porch, tomorrow night, will be a candle burning in a cut-glass vase. If you would come in, pick up the candle and carry it inside. I will wait in darkness, as I don't wish to see other objects. Ordinary things like my teacup do not annoy me but my books and papers, which are everywhere, have become intolerable. I do not wish to see words. Reading even a sentence or two creates an impression that another mind is present, a companion to my thoughts, and I am sick of the illusion; I can touch the page, but no one else is there.

6.2   If you will not come in, then blow out the candle, and quickly leave. Do not speak. Do not explain or apologize.

6.21   We will agree that a capricious wind extinguished the flame.

7   *What we cannot speak about, we must pass over in silence.*

Wittgenstein used to come to see me every evening at midnight, and pace up and down my room like a wild beast for three hours in agitated silence. Once I said to him: "Are you thinking about logic or about your sins?" "Both," he replied, and continued his pacing.

—BERTRAND RUSSELL, *The Autobiography of Bertrand Russell*

Why, then, you may ask, waste time on such insoluble problems? To this one may answer as a historian, or as an individual facing the terror of cosmic loneliness.

—BERTRAND RUSSELL, *A History of Western Philosophy*

A Lit Window Is Someone Awake

I SHOULD TURN off the light.

The lamp is on a table by my bed, a small claw foot table carved by my mother's uncle. At sixty years old, it is one of the youngest pieces of furniture in this house. The house was built in 1881 and furniture has been added, added but seldom subtracted, ever since: a chandelier here, a brass lamp there. Lovely old stuff, lovely old overstuffed stuff. Passed from my great-grandfather to his son to his daughter to her daughter— my sister, Sarah. My younger sister. Wisely married, cleverly pregnant while my mother died. Cleverly with child while I was brilliantly with PhD. "If you'd married first, Harriet, I'd have given the house to you."

Sarah had miscarriages. So did my mother, her first tries. But Sarah is still young, only thirty.

My mother's uncle carved the feet of this table into claws. These are fierce, like a lion's. They are not the claws of a lion, however, because ten inches above the floor the small gouges portraying fur deepen, metamorphose into the fine slanted lines of feathers. This animal might be a griffin, half lion, half bird of prey.

Its twin is in the primary bedroom suite, Sarah and Toby's room. It crouches in the windowed alcove smug as a cat after tuna, holding only lace doilies and small photographs of our mother and father. Doilies unnecessarily protect their table from felt-bottomed frames, while mine is ringed from water glasses and scratched with hastily scribbled equations.

The four of us were roommates for fifteen years—Sarah and I, and the mated tables. We shared a room not for lack of bedrooms, but because our mother believed girls should. She wanted us to whisper in bed, tickle each other, talk of boys and teach each other techniques of mascara application. Perhaps having the two of us share a bed helped our mother imagine that the three empty bedrooms were filled by our older siblings, her miscarriages. Perhaps our lovely, obedient older sisters talked of boys and mascara and giggled late into the night. She called them this, after our father died and there was no one old enough to disapprove; she named them Marilyn, Bonnie, and Ann, and called them our older sisters. She spoke to them. Once she mentioned something Bonnie had said and Sarah was too frightened to sleep, thinking of those girls she had never seen, locked in the other bedrooms. I told her our mother had been making up a story, a fairy tale, like Sleeping Beauty. Poor Sarah. She had more in common with those other sisters. Most nights I read until late and hoped she would be sleeping when I got into bed. But the light from my desk kept her awake. From time to time she sighed, to remind me how she suffered. No matter how I tried to block it, the light kept her awake.

This house seems to fill up, but not to change.

Three months ago one of my students was killed. Pregnancy would have worried me, with our history, but directing a physics thesis seemed safe enough. The miscarriages would only be intellectual: ideas, not blood.

There are points in our lives so delicately balanced, it's impossible not to think that with the smallest nudge, they could have, should have, gone differently. When I close my eyes I see all the seconds of that night: steel girders of the unavoidable resting on accidental threads of spun glass. A bit of glass winks as I click off my office light, half shut the door, remember my jacket, click it on again. Three seconds wink. I can feel the fine cold filament. The weight of a finger would snap it. My thoughts haven't the weight of a breeze; they only stroke it, slide away.

Think of the odds against any moment occurring exactly as it has:

The chance that our experiment would take exactly fourteen hours and thirty-six minutes, ending at 3:20 a.m. Our laser had worked for the first time. Its beam was the medium-blue of Christmas tree lights, the color airports use to mark runways.

The chance that Paul and I would miss the elevator—held on the second floor by a janitor—and walk down three flights of stairs.

The chance that Paul would stop to drink from the water fountain and use the bathroom. That I would wait. That I would offer him a ride home.

I never had before. He lived only four blocks from campus.

Einstein rejected quantum field theory because it implied that nothing could be known with absolute certainty. Every event is merely a probability; nothing is absolutely impossible.

You could appear in my room three seconds from now. You could find yourself in the wood and brass rocking chair between my claw foot table and the window; you could find yourself here mid-rock, believing you were falling backward but only being tilted, gently, in a chair with long curved wooden feet.

Every event is merely a probability; nothing is impossible.

And I wonder how life is different from quantum theory: how anything ever happens. And how, once a thing has happened, the rest of life proceeds as though that thing had always happened.

The chance that we would stop in the corridor to look at photographs of Norbert Wiener. That Paul would repeat one of the most famous stories about him: Wiener standing lost on a street corner, approached by a small girl, giving her an address and asking if she knew which way it was. The girl giggling: "I'll take you home, Daddy."

That Paul would ask if I knew whether the story was true. That I would say I didn't know, but doubted it; we looked at the bearded man expectantly, as if he could tell us.

Paul was my student, but he was not much younger than me.

I should turn off the light.

The lamp is decorated with crystals, triangular prisms suspended from the base of an etched glass globe. In the window are more lead crystals, assorted teardrops and prisms hung at various heights with nylon fishing line. On clear days they throw light in pieces across the room, shards of violet, red, green, yellow. My favorite is the center of indigo and violet, the long, low, slowing end of the spectrum. Light edging into the ultraviolet. Ultraviolet: that is what I call the color suspended beneath indigo. The word is too beautiful to be invisible.

I know this is technically incorrect. I have inverted the spectrum, pretending the fast dark end is slow. But I refuse to think of gentle indigo as faster than red: faster than warning signals and ambulance lights. Faster than blood. Somewhere, a mistake has been made.

It's late, I really must sleep. But as my hand stretches toward the lamp, I notice that its veins are a peculiar vivid blue. I don't remember them being so large, raised so high above the skin. They resist pressure. They are almost firm to my touch.

Both hands are the same. The veins flatten when I hold the hands above my head. They swell again when I lower them.

My feet, lowered to the wood floor, have the same condition as my hands: the veins pop with a blue nearly turquoise, furious and cheerful. And peculiar. But then I am not as familiar with my feet. I can't be certain of what is peculiar, for my feet.

Past the dresser. Past the desk. Stop at the door. Turn. Don't look at your hands. Past the desk. Past the dresser. Past the bed, the empty rocker, the windows.

I have always paced. I paced while on the telephone, for any long call. I never noticed the moment I began, but always at some point the cord stretched as far as it could and I had to turn back. Or my mother would yell, "Sit down! You're making me nervous." I made her nervous, and I ruined the phones. I stretched out the cords so they never coiled as tightly, and I loosened the connection to the receiver so it had to be held in place or it would click, which was annoying. And made my mother nervous.

I paced in my office. Back and forth to the blackboard, taking the chalk with me.

I paced teaching classes, back and forth in front of the long black-board. An idea would erase the students, and I'd be off. I learned to hold on to the podium to make myself stop. Lecture notes would have been a convenient leash, but I never needed them, I had too good a memory.

Sarah won't allow me a blackboard. Chalk dust, you know. And it wouldn't match the quilt. Or perhaps the installation, holes drilled through the flowered wallpaper, would make my stay here seem too permanent. Sarah and Toby won't tell me to leave—I can't be alone yet, and Sarah understands this, she is terrified of being alone—but they tolerate me by believing that soon I'll be myself again. I'll be off to my apartment, where every room looks like a library, so further accommodations aren't necessary.

In place of a blackboard, I tape together sheets of white typing paper, six or eight of them, and lay these on top of the desk. I used to write in pencil, but I've switched to felt-tip markers. Sarah likes buying colored markers. They are cheerful, something she might buy for a child. When the sheets are covered with writing I fold them and stack them with the others, in the bottom drawer of my dresser.

Tonight's sheets are half full. Unlike my office blackboard, there is only one formula: a computation of the tensile strength of a nylon jacket.

Of course everything on the paper is part of some larger formula, some enormous, impossibly unlikely formula.

The chance that we would use the door on Mass Ave rather than the small courtyard exit, though that was closer to my car. The courtyard was too dark, Paul said.

Too dark. That never stopped me before.

The chance that they would drive by—it was a large car, white, old, that's all I remember, I've never paid any attention to cars—during the twenty seconds we walked along Mass Ave.

That they would see us, shadowy between streetlights.

That they would stop.

The chance that the material of the man's jacket would not rip when Paul grabbed hold of it.

There's a knock on my door. Two knocks, not loud, but clear and authoritative: performed precisely, using only the hard top joint of the middle finger. My sister's knock, unchanged since childhood. Un-evolved. The doorknob turns, a faceted cut-glass knob. She would like to open the door without a sound. She turns the knob slowly enough, but the mechanism is old and just before release, it gives a loud click. Still, she tries.

After the click the door opens slowly, not even creaking, and Sarah peeks in. She sees I am up. But then, she already knew I was up; that is why she has come.

"Harriet, it's three in the morning," she says.

"Yes," I say.

"You should try to sleep."

"I should," I say. "I meant to. Oh, did I wake you?"

"Yes, you did. You always do, when you pace like that. I think of burglars. It scares me." She brushes limp sleepy hair out of her eyes, and I study her hands, her veins: flat.

"Probably I would scare off burglars, too," I say. It's a joke, but I suspect it is true.

"Harriet, I'll get you a sleeping pill. Will you take it?"

As she speaks the heat comes on. Water creaks through the old radiators, escaping steam builds from a low-pitched whirring to a higher whistle. We used to pretend the house was firing its jets, preparing to blast off. We were astronauts.

"I don't need it," I say.

"You do need it, you can't sleep. I'll get you more water, too."

"I don't want it."

"Harriet—"

"Rocket fuel," I say to distract her. "Boosters. Zero G." When we were little astronauts she loved these words. She can't have forgotten Old Professor Gravity. My expression is serious, intent, my eyes are wide. I nod as though agreeing with her, raise a finger and shake it thoughtfully, wisely, in front of my face. "Liquid nitrogen, yes, very good."

Sarah backs away from me and huddles into herself. Her arms cross her chest and clutch at each other as if clutching a shawl.

Poor baby sister. Poor Sarah-turtle.

"Burglars," I say. "You know, I never think of burglars. If I woke up to someone tripping over the furniture, it isn't what I would think of first. But you're right, of course, it's the most likely explanation." Sarah thinks I still have a long gray beard. I see this in her hunched turtle neck, turtle shoulders. "You should turn up the heat, if you're cold."

"No, I'm going back to bed."

"Sleep tight. Don't let the burglars bite."

She shivers. "I'm sorry to disturb you, Professor Gravity," she says. "You look so much like my sister. It confuses me."

I almost apologize. But before I can say a word she's gone, blaming me with the back of her head, with her tangled hair as she closes the door, with her rocking footsteps.

She's left me to pace in peace. To pace to pieces.

What bothers Sarah is not that I look like her sister, but that I look like her. Her sister, after all, has never been close to her. No, Sarah is a scientist, like her sister, and the experiment she feeds and checks on nightly—like my roommate in graduate school, a geneticist, devotedly breeding fruit flies—is a copy of herself projected four years into the future. For the past three months our dietary and environmental conditions have been nearly identical, though Sarah does the shopping, and I have greater exposure to colored markers. Thus far my fine brown hair has no invading gray, I have not gained weight, and if I were still on campus, I would frequently be mistaken for an undergrad. Which I would find annoying. Which Sarah would find flattering.

If I did the shopping, I would buy a grandmotherly shade of hair coloring. I would add touches of old age—a few hairs at first, then the temples, all of it in two or three months—and invite Sarah to look further into her future.

Some nights when I finally turned out the reading lamp, Sarah wasn't too sleepy to whisper in the dark. "You're wearing a bra, aren't you?" she said as I was undressing, the first day I wore one. She was eight, I was twelve. She wanted one. I gave her mine, which she wore though she didn't need it. "When did you start your period?" She was eleven, hoping for hers. I had stayed up reading the first volume of Bertrand Russell's autobiography. I copied passages from it into my diary: *After the age of fourteen I found living at home endurable only at the cost of complete silence about everything that interested me.* And, *I did not, however, commit suicide, because I wished to know more of mathematics.* I still remember Russell's insistence that his passion for the girl he would one day marry was not tainted by lust; also that once he finally got up the nerve to kiss her, they spent the entire day kissing, breaking only for lunch and to read aloud from Keats.

Sarah started bleeding at almost the exact age I did: we were one week apart. She has reasons for thinking me an experiment.

My interest in Bertrand Russell may not have been as pure as I pretended at fifteen. I remember reading the passage about kissing several times, and wishing he had said more. Even my crushes were not the kind I could have whispered in the dark to Sarah.

Past the bare white wall, past the desk, past a jar of colored markers. Sometimes, using them, I pretend I'm writing with lasers, and call them by their gases or their wavelengths. Helium-neon, for example, red, for the probabilities assigned to each piece of that night. The chance that Paul would stop to drink from the water fountain: he did this often, but not half the time; say, a third of the time. In red: 1/3.

This number seems justifiable, its explanation simple. Others are harder, or arbitrary, or impossible.

The chance that for the first time, in the shadow between streetlights, Paul would reach for my hand, tug at it to slow me down, turn me toward him. Would he have kissed me?

The chance that a thin young man in blue jeans and a black nylon jacket would jump out of an old white car and grab my purse.

The chance that Paul would try to stop him. The chance that Paul would grab the jacket, would not let go.

It was only a purse. Just pieces of leather, paper, plastic.

The chance that Paul would grab the jacket, would not let go. I pulled on his arms, screamed at him, *Let go!*, hit his hands, hit the man in the black jacket on his head, on his back, screamed for help.

The chance that the man in the black jacket would have a knife. Very likely, given his occupation: 4/5, I wrote in red marker. This estimate may be low.

The chance that he would stab Paul directly in the heart. Leave the knife in him. Run. Jump into the waiting car—the back seat, there was at least one other man, a driver—screech away, cross the bridge into Boston.

Paul gasped and doubled over, sinking, both hands on the knife. He looked up at me, once; he looked terribly confused. As if he didn't know where he was, or what he was doing there.

Past the bed, the claw foot table, the lamp and prisms. Stop at the window. There is a view of streetlights, a wide street with cars parked in every available space. The pavement is yellow-orange, from halogen bulbs. Beyond that, the darkness of Jamaica Pond.

Standing still, and not thinking so loudly, I hear voices: Sarah and Toby. Sarah's is high, whining, childlike. Complaining about me, I suppose. Toby's is softer, consoling, with brief sharper bursts.

I turn off the light. I want to quiet them, put Sarah to sleep.

The moment after the light goes out reminds me of my dark window-less lab, the moment after the lights are off, my hand on a switch, about to start an experiment. Testing and measuring a beam of colored light to see if our computations have successfully predicted that small, tightly controlled portion of the future.

There are footsteps in the hall now, Toby's footsteps, followed by Sarah's. Toby stops by my door but doesn't knock, doesn't move for a minute: listening. He won't wake me, if he thinks I'm asleep. He would rather save whatever Sarah has told him to say for morning.

I haven't moved since I heard their steps, haven't made a sound, and now Toby turns, creaks, and leaves.

The door to their room closes.

I sit in the old rocking chair by the window, but don't rock. The window is full of colored lights. Yellow-orange streetlights, white headlights, red taillights and stoplights, green stoplights. An airplane, low on the horizon: blinking red, steady white.

I have always preferred night to day. In the day there is plenty of light, and plenty of color. At night there are colored lights, and each is intentional, each has meaning. A lit window is someone awake, I told Sarah when we shared a room; she was seven or eight. Moving lights are cars, or airplanes: moving people. A stoplight speaks in color, even when the street is empty. You all will have a chance, it says: now you must wait; now you may go. She had giggled at that, at the idea of a stoplight speaking. But when I pointed to lighted windows, she said, It's so late, what are they all doing? and pulled the curtains. She didn't want to know there were so many lights in the world, awake.

The chair is rocking. Sarah will blame me if she hears it, but it isn't my fault. It's our mother's old chair. It can rock by itself, nervous like the rest of us.

There are stars tonight. It's just dark enough to make them out above the lake.

Paul and I joked once about aiming our laser at the full moon, repeating an experiment that measured its distance from the earth. We imagined our blue light rising against the dark of space—a kiss blown from earth and returned, three heartbeats later, by the ridged ivory moon. Of course we wouldn't have seen this. The moon is too far away. In half a million miles, even light from a laser disperses. Our light would have returned spread invisibly over all of Boston.

True lovers, [the philosopher Agnes Callard] explained, don't really want to be loved for who they are; they want to be loved because neither of them is happy with who he or she is.

—RACHEL AVIV, "Marriage of the Minds"

Distance

The Institute for Elementary Studies

When we met, in 1984, Alex and I were grad students in math at MIT. He was twenty-one at the time, seven years younger than me, but by far the better mathematician, something of a prodigy. There was a family story that on the morning of his fourth birthday, Alex woke up his father and said, "Daddy, you promised to teach me algebra today." His father taught him algebra and his mother taught him French. Somewhere around second grade, the public school teacher gave him zeroes on all his math homework. He didn't show any work, the teacher complained. Of course not: the problems were so simple, Alex did them in his head. His parents, in response, started a private school in Berkeley to accommodate him.

There was a family story about me, too. A few weeks after classes started, my kindergarten teacher called my parents and told them she was afraid I might be retarded. (I was too shy to speak to her. And no one had taught me how to write my name, or tie my shoelaces.) Later, there was the math teacher (trigonometry) who assigned me random bad grades, and the physics teacher who divided my grade by two and didn't notice. I never told my parents about the random grades. My mother's advice to me in high school was to take small steps, speak softly, and always let the boys win.

After our first year at MIT, we spent the month of June at a cabin Alex's family owned near Lake Tahoe—Alex, me, and our friend Mark, an even younger math prodigy. The plan was that each of us would pick an area of math to teach the others. "The Institute for Elementary Studies," Alex called us. We had a portable blackboard and often held classes in the woods.

After being taught to fear math (or math teachers) in high school, I'd avoided it in college, majoring in ethnomusicology (South Indian classical, Javanese gamelan, classical piano). In the course of getting a second, more practical, undergrad degree in computer science, I discovered that I loved reading and solving mathematical proofs. A good proof is beautiful in a way that combines poetry and puzzles, with its own particular brand of suspense, the aha moment of a breakthrough, an insight consistent with everything presented by the arguments thus far, but with a spark, a step dictated by logic but not reached through logic, reached by an intuitive leap that would ultimately be judged not only by its efficiency or its accuracy, but by its elegance. When I read a math textbook, I would go through the proofs step by step like I was reading a mystery novel, trying to guess the murderer before he was revealed. When Alex and Mark read a math book, they would get as far as the theorem, the statement to be proved, then cover up the rest of the page and try to prove it themselves, debating and playing until they either solved the thing or couldn't wait any longer to see how it was done. This was actually thrilling to see. Math was their natural medium. Watching them, sitting on the cabin floor witnessing their combative yet cooperative style of figuring things out, to which I had nothing to contribute, proved to me that however deeply I was able to appreciate it, it wasn't mine.

After classes, we'd hike up into the Superstition Wilderness or down to the lake. It was too cold to swim; the water was just something pretty to look at. There was a rocky beach with a few picnic tables, and at night Alex and I would often go there for some time alone. Also, I was teaching him the stars, seen better above the lake than through all those trees by the cabin. If my Institute for Elementary Studies course had been teaching Alex and Mark the night sky, the constellations and their major stars and the direction to the center of the Milky Way galaxy, *And look*—getting out my binoculars—*see how Sagittarius (shaped like a teapot) is filled with nebulae and star clusters!*—we'd all have been happier.

Star Trek

The picnic table by the lake was a beautiful spot for talking at night, the ink-dark sky of high elevation, the lap of the water, the vast lake with sometimes a moon rising over it. A breeze from the lake blew away the mosquitoes (which flew to the shelter of the trees around the cabin and waited for us). We didn't really drink, at that time, but occasionally we'd split a beer. We imagined things we'd like to do, crazy, unlikely things, and then we'd resolve to do them. Alex and I had already, by this point, decided to take a year off from grad school and live off the land, somewhere in the world. That part, we hadn't figured out yet. It was an idea we'd floated late one night, and then, in the morning, sort of dared each other into: *Well, I would do it. Yeah, well, so would I!*

I was thinking of an island, a warm tropical beach, living by the ocean, which I never got enough of, as time by a beach was always doled out in days, two nights, three nights, on the Florida Panhandle, in the midst of my family's yearly drive to Alabama to visit my mother's family. When I pictured us foraging for food on our warm beach, I pictured us being completely alone, as though we'd discovered a habitable island with no other inhabitants, but plentiful food and fresh water.

And what was Alex thinking? My guess is, he wanted to do something that was hard for him, physically hard, a challenge with some degree of risk. Though Alex wasn't particularly fond of beaches; being near the ocean always made him want to do math. (And there was another thing I was thinking. Not to assume too much, but, if we committed to doing this thing together—another year of preparation, then a year of travel—weren't we committing to each other, as well, even if we didn't actually say so?)

We had lots of *what-if* conversations. What would you do if aliens landed and wanted to take you with them, back to their planet? Would you go? Alex would not. "Not even to learn how aliens do math?" I teased. But Alex was a Platonist: he thought math would be the same, everywhere in the universe.

I most certainly would go. Since the age of ten, the only "job" I'd ever truly wanted was working on a spacecraft like the starship *Enterprise*, traveling to alien worlds. I deeply wanted to meet alien beings. "Because you are one," Alex said. (My mother said the same thing, for different reasons.) The intelligent aliens of my imagination were as unknowable as jellyfish (*If a lion could talk, we would not understand him*, as Wittgenstein wrote) but were always superior, in some vague cosmic moral sense, to humans.

Was I consciously aware of all this when I signed up to audit an undergraduate science-fiction writing workshop for the fall semester? I don't think so. I was interested in the workshop because it was taught by Joe Haldeman, who'd written *The Forever War*, a book I liked, and I'd never heard of a writing workshop; I thought this was a unique opportunity MIT offered its undergrads. I wasn't particularly self-reflective, at the time. I didn't know, or question, why I'd drifted from one field to another, pursuing each new interest with an intensity that resembled a love affair: astronomy to music to computer science to math. A love affair, also, in the way I moved on: when I started a new passion, the old

passion was over. Which is to say, I didn't really know what I wanted
to do, until I started to write. And as soon as I started to write, I was
done with math. I was an MIT dropout.

Seven-card stud

Mark taught us to skip stones. We got into the habit of collecting
skipping stones, flattish, thinnish smooth stones that we carried around
in our pockets and then piled near the picnic table. Alex taught us to
play poker. Seven-card stud was his game of choice. We played in the
cabin a few nights for practice. Then we went to Reno, an hour's drive,
to play in a casino. Mark wasn't old enough to enter a casino legally, but
he looked it. Both Mark and Alex had full beards, so no one questioned
them. I was the one who looked too young, at twenty-eight, to buy a
bottle of wine.

Though I knew the basics of poker—to ante at the start, how to bid,
the ranks of all the hands, what beat what and how likely you were to
draw it—I had never played with competitive players, with real money
to lose. We played at a table with the lowest bids, one to three dollars,
but that was still a lot of money for me. At the seven-card stud tables,
there were seven players plus a dealer. Alex sat behind me, massaging
my shoulders. My opponent, for the hour I played, was a large man with
diamond rings on several fingers. Large diamonds. He liked to raise,
no matter what. Alex hadn't taught me the psychology of poker, only
the rules of the game and how the betting worked.

The first round of seven-card stud is two face-down cards and one
card face up that everyone can see. I was dealt three tens, two hidden.
Everyone looked at their cards as surreptitiously as they could, turning
up the corner of each card just enough to see its suit and number. I was
paranoid about my glasses reflecting the cards to the other players, so I
had to look at them a couple times to make sure what I thought I saw
was actually there. My three of a kind was midrange. There was risk.
Diamond Rings bid high from the start. That's what he always did, I
gradually figured out; he wanted there to be something in the pot after

he'd bullied everyone else out of the game. I knew not to back out when I started with three of a kind. And by the end of the game, I had a full house. A pair showed up on the very last card. By then, everyone but me had folded. And Diamond Rings raised every single round. And I called him, again and again, and I won. And while I knew a full house was likely to beat anything Diamond Rings had, by the end I was shaking, could not stop shaking, and Alex was trying to hide this from the others as best as could, draping himself across my shoulders as if he just couldn't get enough of me.

For Alex's birthday, we drove to a beach warm enough for swimming. There was a full-circle rainbow-hued sun dog around the sun. *Of course there's a sun dog on Alex's birthday*, I thought. *He's that lucky.* Years later I found a bit of our picnic table conversation in a notebook. Alex, one of the most confident people I've ever met, said that if he'd had my obstacles—meaning, my parents and my teachers—he didn't think he could have succeeded. I'd forgotten he said this, and was surprised by it. But even at the time, I didn't believe it.

Tahiti, Bora Bora, Fatu-Hiva, New Zealand, Australia

After our second year at MIT, Alex and I took a year off to travel to Fatu-Hiva, in the Marquesas, one of the most remote islands in the South Pacific. "That's the stupidest thing I've ever heard! You'll destroy your career!" said the chairman of the Math Department. To Alex, not to me. But in fact, it helped his career. He submitted papers to math journals with postmarks from all over the South Pacific, covered with exotic stamps, and his return address was always *Post Restante.* Everywhere we went, we worked—him on math, me on my first short stories. Though this wasn't a form of "work" recognized by the villagers of Omoa, on Fatu-Hiva, the island where we went to try to live off the land, the original reason we'd taken that year off.

We reached Fatu-Hiva after six weeks of travel. Once there, we explored a bit, hiking the spectacular trail along the spine of the island to its other town, Hanavave, or swimming on the black sand beach. I swam in a tee shirt and pants cut off just below my knees because a month before, two French women had been forced to leave the island after they swam and sunbathed topless. Now the villagers wanted women to be covered from shoulders to knees. But most of our days were spent sitting at a picnic table on the second story of a termite-eaten house we rented from the village *gendarme* for six dollars a night, writing in our notebooks, the notebooks in which we'd intended to record our experiences living off the land.

The villagers watched us on our balcony above the main street, sitting at the picnic table, doing, as far as they could tell, absolutely nothing. "Why did you come to Fatu-Hiva?" they asked us, in the simple French they spoke with outsiders. It was a good question. *"C'est tres jolie,"* we would answer. It's very pretty.

Our first week on the island one of our neighbors, the village priest, invited us to lunch, proud that he was about to travel to Fiji to meet with Pope John Paul, who was touring the South Pacific. During lunch I asked, in my wobbly French, if anyone there remembered Thor Heyerdahl's book *Fatu-Hiva*. In the 1930s, the Norwegian adventurer Heyerdahl and his very accommodating young wife had researched islands around the world and settled on Fatu-Hiva as their best option for primitive survival. It had year-round water, abundant fruit and fish, no large predators, and no horrible diseases now that elephantiasis and leprosy were under control (*the six major diseases of the natives—the common cold, influenza, tuberculosis, elephantiasis, venereal disease and leprosy, were all unknown before the white man came*). We understood that every fruit tree on the island was owned by someone, and we'd brought a well-hidden stash of their colorful currency, intending to rent a small piece of land on the unpopulated side of the island. Much as Heyerdahl had done.

The cash was a small pile, easy to hide, because Alex was fascinated with bills of large denominations. Most of the bills he carried were worth the equivalent of roughly $120, beautiful things decorated on the back with an engraving of tropical fish. More experienced travelers would carry smaller bills. On Tahiti and Bora Bora and Mooréa, there were mornings we couldn't even buy a coffee, because the vender didn't have change. Only a bank could break those things, and where we were going, there weren't any banks. But to apply for the yearlong visa to French Polynesia, we had to open a bank account there. A useless bank account full of colorfully engraved fish.

We read Heyerdahl's book as confirmation of our own research, the anthropologists and art historians and various wanderers we'd interviewed and asked, *Where would you go?* Heyerdahl and his wife spent the last weeks of their time on Fatu-Hiva hiding in a cave, waiting for the copra boat to arrive and rescue them. The book told stories of finding a pregnant scorpion in their thatched hut, put there as a prank, and poisonous centipedes placed in their beds. I figured times had changed. They hadn't.

When I mentioned Heyerdahl, the men at lunch laughed so hard they slapped the table in glee. "Every hippie in Europe read that book! They think they can come here and mangos will fall into their laps!" They placed bets on how long the hippies would survive. Like traders shorting stocks, they wanted them to fail. And we were the hippies.

This was one of our strengths as a couple, and also one of our weaknesses: that we could imagine doing something as difficult as living off the land for a year on a remote island in the South Pacific, then follow through with eighteen months of research and preparation—studying French, learning wilderness first aid, applying for visas, constantly scrimping to save enough money—when the thing we were trying so hard to do was not really suited to us, not something that, in the end, on the real-world Fatu-Hiva, we would actually want to do.

Distance

In the fall of 1993, Alex and I moved to different cities. Alex went to Minneapolis for a semester-long workshop on probability theory. I went to St. Louis to start an MFA in fiction. It was the first time we'd lived apart, and I want to say, though I'm not entirely certain of this, that neither of us expected the separation to be permanent.

Permanent already seems like the wrong word to use. What about us ever felt permanent? In nine years together, besides Fatu-Hiva, we'd lived in Cambridge, Berkeley, Ithaca, Corvallis, and Madison. By the time we reached Ithaca, Alex's fellowship year at Cornell, we half-jokingly agreed not to make any new friends, because friends were people we were always immediately leaving. In Corvallis, or really Philomath (the perfect name: *a lover of learning, especially mathematics*), twenty miles or so from the Oregon State campus, we bought eight acres of land and fantasized about building a house. I drew large and impractical designs, impractical not only because of money, which we didn't have, but because my fantasy of a house wasn't suited to Oregon weather, to nine months of rain. It was a design for living outside, with large open balconies and long colonnades connecting the rooms. I never believed we would build that impractical house, but the land itself—three acres of meadow sloping uphill from a little stream to five acres of forest, real forest, giant old pines, moss, ferns, lichen-covered boulders—I immediately loved. Then Alex decided to take a job in Madison, instead, and we sold it.

I remember the time spent looking for new apartments, driving across the country, learning my way around each new place, more vividly than the months we'd sort of live somewhere. We'd find a good dentist and a veterinarian for our cat and a favorite café. Then we'd be moving again, half our boxes still packed and ready to go.

Italian lessons

At the end of his time in Minneapolis, Alex spent the night with Sonia, a mathematician from Milan. They lay in bed naked, but didn't have sex. That's what Alex liked, at the time, what turned him on—the thrill of mutual attraction expressed physically through affection rather than sex. Spending an evening walking around Cambridge holding hands with a woman from the MIT chorus he'd had a crush on for months. Flirting with a woman he'd offered a ride from Oregon to Berkeley, driving for hours with her hand on his shoulder, massaging or just resting.

That was perfect, Sonia emailed the next day. Alex wrote back, *Can we do it again tonight?* Sonia was so disappointed she almost said no; she thought he wanted sex, after all. But he didn't. They spent another night cuddling and pointing to things and speaking only Italian.

Alex told me about Sonia the next evening, after I picked him up at the St. Louis airport. We were driving back to my apartment in the dark. I've often wondered why dark cars make such good confessionals. Is it because one person, the person driving, can't look at the other? "So," he started. "Did *you* make it through the semester?" I knew what he meant. "Yes," I said. "I didn't," he said. Maybe he felt guilty, a little, but he also couldn't wait to tell me about it.

How to explain myself

Spring semester, the class I was most excited about was "Seminar on the Sentence," taught by William Gass, a writer I greatly admired and was afraid of, those two emotions, admiration and fear, being deeply linked in me. I was a night owl and hated early classes, but that semester I also audited an 8 a.m. course Gass taught in the Architecture Department, on "The Window." I would make a thermos of coffee and sit in the dark in the huge lecture hall watching a slideshow of windows from every part of the world, mostly photos Gass had taken himself, with his amplified voice telling their stories, stories about place and form, literal and figurative interpretations of the ways light can be let into a room. In every session, moments of the sublime. A woman standing in a window on a street in Amsterdam at night holding twins, one small well-swaddled baby on each arm, right up against the full-length, ground-floor window, smiling at people who passed her on the sidewalk only a foot away. As though her living room was an extension of public space, with no American sense of privacy, our thick curtains drawn at dusk lest someone see in.

The "Seminar on the Sentence" met once a week in the living room of Gass's large, elegant home. One evening, early in the semester, I argued against the interpretation of Ludwig Wittgenstein in a presentation made by one of the other grad students. We'd been assigned to read two sections of his *Tractatus Logico-Philosophicus*. I'd first read the *Tractatus* while in high school. Somehow, the tiny Newburgh bookstore had a copy of it, which I bought because I liked the way it looked on the page. I loved the short numbered statements with spaces between them for thinking. The possibilities of fragments excited me. I already knew that much, that I was drawn to fragments, his, or Nietzsche's in *The Gay Science*, which I read sitting at the counter in Perkins Pancake House with coffee and a slice of Boston cream pie, skipping classes, yet again. If I didn't always know exactly what Wittgenstein was saying, I had some notion of what he *wasn't* saying. In class I defended him, perhaps a bit possessively, too passionately, from this woman who pronounced his name "Wittgensteen."

"You just dropped an atomic bomb on an undeveloped nation," a friend told me after class. I say *a friend*, though this was a man I didn't know well. Still, he was one of the few grad students connected to the writing program who didn't actively dislike me. After Alex came to class with me one night, this man asked, "How does it feel to be married to someone so good-looking?" Oddly, from the back, this man looked exactly like Alex. They were both six foot one and had shortish black hair. That night, they both wore black jeans and black leather jackets. I had no idea what to say to him. This was frequently true. In too many social situations, I either said nothing or said the wrong thing, then let the wrong thing stay in the air because I didn't know yet how to explain myself, how to apologize and try again, how to pin down, corner, what I had actually meant. I was shy, too shy, but it was more than that. However, I wasn't shy about speaking in class, where my direct style and harsh voice—

It was at this time, when I was thirty-seven years old, that I started to understand how other people perceived me. My voice, in class—someone finally told me—sounded angry when I wasn't. Or sounded condescending when what I felt was uncertain. Or sounded angry and condescending when what I felt was excited and generous. I was deaf in my right ear, so I always spoke too loudly. I had terrible allergies, which over the years made my voice more nasal and more forced. Also, my opinions were too strong. Also, my utter lack of attention to personal style. Long, untrimmed mousy-brown hair in a ponytail; tee shirts and jeans, sweaters so old that some had belonged to my father (who died nine years earlier) and were full of moth holes. No makeup. Thick, thick glasses, as I was extremely nearsighted, so that my eyes, if they could be seen at all, looked tiny.

When we first met, Alex often walked the halls of MIT barefoot. The soles of his feet were dark and calloused, his toenails thick as claws from repeated injuries. He played ultimate Frisbee barefoot in the grassy main courtyard. He would do anything for a save, jump-dive any distance. After games he'd have grass-stained scrapes along his arms and legs, but he was happy to have run full-out and exhausted himself. I always thought his face was beautiful—his father was Indian, his mother Hungarian, and he had an exotic look, hard to place, skin the color of a permanent tan, almond eyes, thick lashes, thick black hair, a thick, shaggy beard. He still had a beard, nine years later, but now he trimmed it. And his clothes fit. When Ethan asked how it felt to be married to someone so good-looking, it took me a while to realize what he might have meant, what some part of him may have been thinking: Why was Alex with *me*?

The go-between

Our second year at UW–Madison, Alex was awarded a research grant from the National Science Foundation for half a million dollars. It was shocking to hear of so much money. An amazing break for anyone, but especially for a twenty-nine-year-old, nontenured math professor. When Alex called from his office to tell me, my heart skipped a beat— half a million dollars! But the terms of the grant specified that we, that is, Alex, got nothing. He was in charge of the money, but could only spend it on other people. Other mathematicians.

Alex had a sabbatical scheduled for the spring semester, and our plan had been for him to join me in St. Louis. But that changed after the grant. He had to stay in Madison, he had to start using the money. We'd given up our apartment when he left for Minneapolis and I left for St. Louis, so he sublet a furnished house and invited Benjamin, a mathematician from Stanford, who was also on sabbatical, to come and share it and do math with him.

One of Benjamin's goals for his semester off was to find a wife, or at least a serious girlfriend. He quickly got hooked into a network that organized social events for single professors. And at the first event, he met someone. She was blonde. She was beautiful. She had a PhD in political science from Stanford. As Alex put it, Benjamin fell in love with Maria when he'd known her for about ten seconds. Benjamin was one of Alex's best math friends, and good-looking, but socially, he was rigid and extremely nerdish. After a couple dates, Maria started to express some doubts. Instead of making out when he dropped her off after dinner, as they had at first, they sat in his car, engine running to keep the heat on, and had hour-long debates about their compatibility.

Benjamin, in a fit of ill-considered desperation, asked Alex to talk to Maria, to argue his case. Alex, though skeptical, agreed to have lunch with her. *She really is great*, he emailed me afterward. We'd been wondering how a charming, beautiful woman could be serious about Benjamin. It turned out she wasn't. She was trying to figure out how to convince him she'd lost interest. She asked Alex to help her. Now he was, in theory, acting as a character witness for Benjamin to woo Maria, while at the same time helping Maria plan a gentle, but firm, breakup with Benjamin. Alex thought he ought to feel guilty, but actually he enjoyed this, especially the emails with Maria, who reported back regularly and in flirty detail her cleverly discouraging replies to Benjamin's persistent messages. She passed along arguments she found amusing, such as his claim that she didn't know him well enough to turn him down. And then Alex would hear Benjamin's version of this, the earnestness with which he believed it.

In late February, Benjamin left town for a week. Alex took advantage of his absence to throw a large party, inviting all the grad students in the Math Department. We'd done this each year we lived in Madison, once hiring a jazz band, once putting a crown of tinsel stars on every student as they entered our apartment. They were great parties. And Alex invited Maria. And late that night, on the living room carpet, in front of a Slovenian grad student passed out drunk in an armchair, Alex and Maria started making out. Making out with someone in a dress, a short, loose dress, was a novelty. Possibly a revelation. "Such easy access," as Alex put it.

Thirty days

Alex set a time limit to his affair with Maria: thirty days. He told me this over the phone after the first night he slept with her. Maria couldn't be a one-night stand. He wanted to get to know her, spend time with her. Take her out on dates. We'd both had crushes (Alex's mode) or lusts (my mode) during our years together. But however much we'd crushed and lusted, in the four years we'd been married, neither of us had slept with anyone else. Sonia was the closest thing. Alex loved games; he was an excellent card player. He'd invented card games only the two of us knew. Games always had rules. Games were, on a basic level, defined by their rules. Maybe he thought, at least in the beginning, that making up a rule made the affair more like a game. Something with an ending. (But also with winners and losers.)

Did I believe feelings could be told they had a use-by date? Did I expect everything to go back to normal, at least our new normal, living apart while trying to keep our lives together, after thirty days of romantic trysts with Maria? No. But I wasn't going to tell Alex not to do something he clearly was going to do anyway. Maybe I could have stopped him if I'd been living with him in Madison, if seeing Maria meant leaving me at home and coming back to me late at night or the next morning, from her bed, having to abruptly change personality, modes of being. If I'd been there, I would have resented his ecstasies.

"She's the first person I've gone out with as an adult," Alex said, on a weekend visit to St. Louis. I said, "Yeah, you were still growing when I met you." Which was literally true.

That weekend we booked tickets to Europe for the summer. Alex was invited to conferences in Sweden, Germany, and Italy. We'd be traveling for six weeks, thousands of miles from Madison, thousands of miles from Maria.

Our second year in Madison, one of my favorite writers, John Coetzee, was in residence for a month. Alex and I both took his seminar, and he read several of my stories. He was encouraging, but, "Your characters are too nice to each other," he said. The next time I saw him, at a conference in St. Louis, I told him Alex was still living back in Madison. "Marriage wasn't meant for that," he said.

Maria vs. Sharon

1. Maria has a good job; hence, Alex would not be supporting her.
2. Maria owns a house.
3. Maria dresses well.
4. Maria has friends in Madison and wants to stay there.
5. Everyone tells him how pretty Maria is.
6. Maria isn't at risk of losing her eyesight before the age of fifty. I was diagnosed with a hard-to-control type of glaucoma when I was thirty-one, a few months after our return from the South Pacific. And Alex was supportive. Always. Another thing he had to support.
7. I'm going to leave sex out of this. But of course, sex cannot be left out.
8. "She's not as smart as you," Alex told me, several times a week. This was supposed to make me feel better. Later, Alex would say, "Does it surprise you that I want to be with someone less intelligent than you?"
9. Maria wants kids.

If these were elements of a weighted equation, the multiplier for 9 would be so high it would reduce the other factors to the significance of round-off errors.

Tractatus Logico-Eroticus

I met Sam my first week of grad school. He was a postdoc in the Philosophy Department who taught one of my classes, a graduate seminar on consciousness. That first week, I had a huge list of classes to check out, within the English Department and, mostly, outside of it, as I wanted to write about things other than books that people had already, in my opinion, written too much about. "A Theory of Consciousness" sounded about right: cutting-edge, unsettled philosophy; the nature of man; maybe even (panpsychism) the nature of the universe.

For the first class, the professor showed up late—young, long-haired, nerdishly cute—with a crazy story of dropping a huge box of packing peanuts down the stairs of his apartment building, then feeling morally obliged to pick up every last one of them. Even if he'd be late for class. If you need to charm ten people you don't know into forgiving you, it really helps to have an Australian accent. After half an hour of listening to him explain packing peanuts and the nature of consciousness, I had a crush on him.

I teased Alex that Sam was the first person I'd met since MIT who was as smart as he was. Alex liked a challenge, so sometimes when he visited me he'd go to Sam's seminar and debate topics he barely knew about as vigorously as the most ambitious and well-read grad students. Both of them enjoyed this. They became friends.

But now, Alex was sleeping with Maria, and Sam was no longer my professor. And the more I thought about Sam, the more I wanted to sleep with him. But this wasn't going to just happen. I'd been his student; I was married; he liked my husband. I'd have to make an obvious move, I'd have to seduce him. To accomplish this, I resorted to philosophy, to Wittgenstein's *Tractatus*. I wrote my own *Tractatus*, just for him. Sam's favorite movie, at that time, was *Groundhog Day*. An alarm (digital, with giant green letters) would go off at 6:00 a.m., and Bill Murray's one day to try to get everything exactly right would start over, and over, and over.

Wittgenstein	6	*This is the general form of a proposition.*
Me	*6:00*	*This is the general form of a proposition:*
		I would like to sleep with you.

For the remainder of my four-page riff on Wittgenstein, that line came up again and again, resetting to 6:00 a.m., like the movie. Like my brain. I felt myself becoming obsessed.

I printed off my *Tractatus Logico-Eroticus* and taped it to the door of Sam's apartment exactly at 6 p.m., for luck. I knew he wouldn't be there; he was always in his office or at a movie until late. The rest of the night I sat by my computer, checking email every minute. He wrote to me after midnight. *Very well organized. And some quite attractive arguments. Though, perhaps you haven't sufficiently developed the moral aspects of your proposition?*

Sam needed a few days to get used to the idea, but in the end, he agreed. We picked a night, the night of the Academy Awards. Sam, like Wittgenstein, loved movies. Whenever his writing wasn't going well, he went to a multiplex. If there wasn't a movie he wanted to see, he would buy a random ticket, then dart into and out of theaters until he found an actress cute enough or a plot appealing enough to keep his attention. So while I had seen almost none of the films nominated, Sam had seen some part of almost all of them.

Sam knocked on the door to my apartment that night looking like he always looked, with his long, tangled hair, and dressed, as always, in black sweatshirt, jeans, and sneakers. I didn't know what to say to him. My obsessive imaginings had skipped this part, going directly to bed. I was happy to pretend he was there just to watch television. "It's starting right now!" I said. Then I ran into the kitchen to get him a glass of white wine. Our conversation, during the commercial breaks, was all about Alex and Maria, a topic which fascinated Sam in a soap-opera-ish kind of way: he was intensely curious about what would happen next.

Each of us waited for the other to make a move, sitting side by side on my futon sofa-bed, in front of the television, wondering how

I'm-attracted-to-you-but-is-this-really-okay would be magically trans-
formed into sexual passion. There were some awkward minutes when,
at my suggestion, we converted the sofa-bed to a bed-bed. We adjusted
the pillows, then continued watching. The truth is, I've never liked
having sex with people I haven't touched before, people with whom I
haven't gradually built up a ready-to-explode sense of sexual tension.
It wasn't right for either of us, and yet I didn't regret it. I stayed awake
all night, thrilled that Sam was there in bed next to me. Can you invite
a man to just spend the night in bed with you instead of inviting him
to have sex? You can, but even after Alex and Sonia, I didn't consider
that. It wasn't what I thought I wanted.

New Harmony

The first week of April, Alex was invited to a small conference in New
Harmony, Indiana, a town that had been home to several utopian com-
munities in the 1800s. I joined him for a night. It was three hours away
but an easy drive from St. Louis, and its utopian history appealed to
both of us. A place for new beginnings. A place with interesting ghosts.

A few days before this, a friend had given him some pot, a rolled
joint. Alex was thirty and had never smoked pot. He didn't expect to
like it, and had previously avoided it so as not to screw up his brain for
doing math. Now he was in a frame of mind where trying new things
had its own appeal. Even the fact that he'd be crossing state borders
with an illegal drug appealed to him: he was tired of doing the right
thing. I had smoked pot only once, when I was eighteen. Or, not literally smoked it, but had it blown into my mouth by my boyfriend, who
would take a puff, hold it in his mouth, cover my mouth with his, and
release the filtered smoke as I tried to suck it down to my lungs. It was
more like kissing than smoking, until the pot started to take effect. An
invisible box formed around me and shut me in. I'd inhaled claustro-
phobia. All I wanted to do was lie on the couch in his basement and
wait for the feeling to go away. But now, like Alex, I was restless, angsty,
and wanted to try it again.

In the end, Alex forgot to bring the joint, which made both of us sad. We needed something outside ourselves to focus on, to experience together. We could have gotten drunk, instead—Alex almost never drank, this also would have been a novelty—but I hadn't brought anything alcoholic with me, and at dinner, when we asked if there was a liquor store nearby, someone told us the town was dry.

His thirty days with Maria were up that week. They would have dinner one last time, one last night together. The next day, he would leave for a conference in Toronto. He'd bought a new shirt to wear for that night, because I'd bought all the dress shirts he owned and suddenly, he didn't feel right wearing a shirt I'd bought on a date with her. He tried on the new shirt to show me, to make sure I liked it, to make sure it looked good on him. It did; everything looked good on him.

Sam and I had agreed to spend only one night together, a one-off, as he put it, a phrase I'd never heard before and didn't like. I hadn't seen him much since then. I was getting over him, a feeling like floodwaters receding, which was a relief and made me happier to be meeting up with Alex. On my way to New Harmony, I stopped by campus to go to a talk a friend was giving in the Philosophy Department. Sam was there. Seeing him was like being injected with heroin, or something more addictive. He was standing in front of the room, waiting to introduce my friend. He waved at me uncomfortably and looked relieved that I didn't walk over to sit near him. I waved back, then left before the talk started.

Driving to meet Alex, Sam was all I thought about. How the sight of him had altered everything. Against my will. As though I had no will. Alex knew exactly how I felt. We wanted and we didn't want these feelings. He wanted them for just a few more days, and then—? And I, finally, didn't want them, and experienced this resurrection of lust, or obsession, or whatever it was, as an assault.

We were in remarkably similar states of mind: distracted by our lovers, not knowing what was going to happen or what we wanted to happen, not knowing what to do with the intensity of everything. After dinner, we left our room and walked through the campus for hours. I think it was drizzling. I don't remember anything about the place at night except large wet lawns and large dark dripping trees and fog that may have been inside of me. He talked about Maria. I talked about Sam. We talked like, we didn't talk like, a married couple: we talked like best friends.

We wandered about in the dark, getting wet, or maybe we had an umbrella, there was always an umbrella in the back of my old Volvo. We wandered about in the dark, each of us gripping the handle of the umbrella, walking in step, close together, to stay dry. Pulled together and apart. What should we do. What could we do. When we had sex that night we used condoms Alex had bought for Maria, lambskin condoms, because she was allergic to latex.

Alex said the grant had changed him. That week, he'd gone to the chairman of the Math Department at Madison and asked for a raise. Without first talking to me and strategizing, without first telling me.

Alex was so young when we first met. Puppyish. He *bounced*, running barefoot out of a building, down the steps, to meet me.

The next morning, as we stood in line at the cafeteria to order breakfast, we heard that Kurt Cobain had killed himself. My first thought was, *No, this already happened, he didn't die.* But this time, he was dead.

Driving too fast

A week later, Alex sent email from the conference in Toronto: he'd changed his plane ticket and was coming to see me instead of flying back to Madison. *Great*, I wrote back. There was a student production of *Hair* outside in the main quad, I'd seen it the weekend before, he'd love it, we could drive there straight from the airport.

I met him at the arrival gate. He hugged me and told me he was drunk. He wouldn't answer questions, just shook his head. Walking to the car he took my hand, gripping it much too hard. I had a tape cued on the car stereo that I wanted him to hear, The Cure, *Kiss Me, Kiss Me, Kiss Me.* "Turn it off," he said. I still thought we were going to *Hair*, but no, he wanted to go straight home.

We walked in, sat down at the dining room table. He took both my hands in his. Gripping them much too hard. "I've decided I must leave you," he said. The words sounded like he was saying them aloud after saying them in his head for hours and hours and hours. "I have to see her again."

I have no memory of what I said to him, or of anything either of us said or did the rest of that night. I remember clearly the airport, the drive home, sitting at the table, his too-tight grip, his words. After that: nothing.

I had several days to get used to the fact that this person was not the person I'd walked with for hours in the rain, only a week ago. The next day was Saturday and we drove up to Madison. Alex drove. He drove too fast, another thing he never did. It was risky and it felt right. This was the world now—risks would be taken to match its intensity. We drove to the rented house. Where Benjamin lived. There wasn't any food in the house; both of them had been at the conference in Toronto, and Benjamin suggested that we all go out to dinner. Alex couldn't say no. He couldn't speak.

Alex sat next to me in the restaurant, across from Benjamin. I tried to do all the talking, asking Benjamin this and that about the conference, about Toronto, but Benjamin wanted to talk about Maria. She wouldn't return his calls. She wouldn't return his emails. He said he knew they could work things out, but she had to give him a reasonable chance! Alex was looking around the restaurant in a panic, breathing through his mouth. He got up and left the table without saying anything. I wondered if he would come back. He did. He had gone to a pay phone and called Maria. She had a plan: They would tell Benjamin together. Yes, she was sure. That was the only way to do it. Alex came back to the table. He could breathe again.

Menagerie

I stayed two nights in Madison. Alex and I shared his bed, which had never been my bed, this bed in his rented house. We lay awake side by side late into the night, holding hands. "What will you do?" he said. I had no idea, not yet. I hadn't planned an escape hatch. Talking in the dark, holding hands, the love we still felt came out late at night, headbutting the new love. I said things like, *Why does a new love have to end the old one? Why does it replace it? Love should be additive, it should accumulate.* He agreed with me, in theory, but that wasn't how he felt.

I told Alex I wanted to meet Maria. He didn't object. Probably he was eager to see her, too.

He called her the next morning and set up a meeting for that afternoon. On the drive to her house, I watched Alex's face change, the sad muscles unclench, the happy muscles engage. Maria, when she came to the door, also looked happy in a way that didn't take my presence into account. She was, as I'd expected, very pretty. She was several inches taller than me, slim-hipped and fine-boned in a way that gave her an elegant look I would never have. She wore a pink button-down cardigan and slim white jeans. I was dressed the way I always dressed when I was nervous and didn't know what to wear: in clothes that I thought made me look thinner, even if they didn't quite match or didn't make sense for the time of year, a burnt-orange sleeveless knit vest and dark green jeans. A fall outfit in April.

We sat down on opposing couches in her living room, Alex and Maria on one side, me on the other. She served black tea and madeleines. Alex and Maria couldn't stop smiling at each other. Of course, I'd actually forgotten: they hadn't seen each other since Alex left for Toronto. They hadn't seen each other since they'd broken up, and now they were going to be together.

From the living room couch I could see a long sideboard in the dining room, covered with glass terrariums and cages. "I'm going to look at your animals, okay?" I said. I wasn't going to leave Alex and Maria alone for the rest of the afternoon, I wasn't quite that generous, I would drive back to St. Louis the next day, as planned. But I went into the other room, with my back to them, giving them a moment to, whatever. She had the kind of menagerie a kid might have: a large iguana, painted turtles, hamsters, a tank of fish. She also, Alex told me the night before, had two cats and an aging collie, deaf and almost blind. The collie was sleeping on a cushion in the corner of the living room. The cats were hiding. "Do they all have names?" I'd asked. Yes, even the fish. Ivan, the green iguana, was my favorite. Ivan the Terrible Wonderful, or something like that. He lived in a terrarium decorated with smooth stones and tree branches. His thick-lidded orange eye was just beyond the glass of his cage, and he seemed to be watching me. The crest along his back lifted when I walked over, then flattened.

It was easy to picture kids in this house, asleep in the extra bedrooms. Letting the iguana out of its heated cage to show it off to friends. Banging on the grand piano.

This is what it came to, in the end, why some part of Alex kept an eye out for crushes and why, year after year, in all of my dreams, I was single. I didn't want kids. This was the conditional that haunted our love: Would I change? Would he? That year I'd started to reconsider, to reimagine our life with kids. But it was too late.

The names of streets didn't mean anything

I drove from Madison back to St. Louis, took the usual exit from the freeway, and got lost. There were so many roads. All of them were gray. I pulled into a parking lot and looked around the car for something with my address on it, but I'd cleaned out the dead mail and used tissues before driving up to Madison. The registration, the insurance still said Wisconsin. I would have to call someone. To ask where I lived. I'd have to find a phone booth and remember all the numbers correctly, enter them perfectly, then hope the person I called was home to answer their phone. This felt impossible. So I sat in the car and drank water until I could picture my street, my first-floor apartment, the wide brick porch and the flowers I'd planted in front.

I walked into my apartment and turned on the computer, as I always did. I dialed into the server, the modem screeching as though it had something urgent to tell me. But there was nothing, no new messages.

Before this, Alex had always sent some friendly thing for me to read at the end of my drive, what he was cooking for dinner, how much he already missed me. But today, freed of me, Alex was . . . preoccupied.

I stood by the computer, looking around the apartment. What did I do here?

I opened a bottle of wine. I couldn't tell if I was hungry. I sat at the dining room table, a green cast-aluminum table meant to be patio furniture. It had an ornate leafy design with a hole in the center for an umbrella. Crumbs dropped through, but I liked it. I sat at the table, which was cold and solid, and drank several glasses of wine. I never did this. When I was alone drinking wine, I sat outside on the front steps watching fireflies. Or sat on the porch and read. Or sat at my desk and read or wrote.

The light over the table was too bright. It took me an hour to realize this. There was a box of matches on the table. There was a candle. I lit the candle and set it on the mantel above the fireplace, turned off all the other lights. In this shadow light I was drawn to shells on the mantel, shells collected in Florida the year before, when my sisters and my aunts gathered for my mother's seventieth birthday. The red scallop had a dried seahorse inside it about an inch long. Its eyes were missing, but what filled the sockets looked exactly like eyes, black centers.

Why was I so . . . is there a word for this? Living in suspended animation. The feeling that a character in a claymation movie might have, as it awaits the next arrangement of its material, which is its body and its world.

What my husband told me about the woman he is in love with

Once, late at night, they walked naked down the street, calling for her lost cat.

He sat on the hood of her car while she drove to a party.

He likes the way she talks to her animals.

My brain learned to make LSD

Five days later, on a Friday afternoon, the last day of classes, I was looking at the bookshelf next to my bed, not at any particular book but in the general direction of the bookshelf, when a rush of chemicals flooded my brain, replacing every sad, lost neuron in it with an ecstatic one. I stood there in a state of sudden bliss. My perspective, my location in the universe, had slipped partway into a world parallel to ours in which I could sense the different paths my life might take. I was comforted. I was elated. My mind absorbed the ecstasy, the biochemical disruption my brain had made for itself, while thinking, *This is so fucking weird.*

My final paper for the "Seminar on the Sentence" was due that Monday. The assignment was to analyze a single sentence. Mine was from a story by Guy Davenport, the writer whose sentences I loved the most:

Wasps fly backward in figure eights from their paper nests memorizing with complex eye and simple brain the map of colors and fragrances by which they can know their way home again, in left-hand light that bounces through right-hand light, crisscross.

The sentences of my paper channeled both Davenport and Gass:

The sentence is a flight of figure eights, explaining how the wasp navigates, which is by polarized light, described in the eight-word phrase that is itself a figure eight: light bouncing left, and right, and crossing. *Crisscross* is the wasp-waist of the eight. And wasps are eight-shaped, without their wings.

The argument from putting-up-with

I turned in my paper, then drove up to Madison. It was a six-hour drive, plenty of time to argue with Alex in my head. There was the argument from having put up with so much while he established his career: moving every year for five years in a row, always from one side of the country to the other, MIT to Berkeley to Cornell to Oregon to Wisconsin. Repeatedly putting yourself into situations where you have no prospects of jobs or friends only makes sense as a long-term strategy when the person for whom you've made these sacrifices doesn't abandon you.

Then there was the argument from putting up with stuff Maria would never have put up with, such as, the table manners of the younger Alex. The first time he met one of my oldest friends, we had a picnic lunch. There was a moment when Cindy was reaching over to cut a piece of butter for her baguette, and just before her knife reached it, Alex picked up the whole stick of butter and bit into it, scraping off a layer of butter with his teeth. Cindy froze, her knife suspended inches from the butter. She no longer wanted it. Instead of apologizing, Alex insisted that he was just being "efficient."

None of this mattered. Nothing I had put up with, nothing he had put up with, nothing we had done together. Kids trumped all arguments. I knew that. I knew that. But this, also, I blamed on Alex. Who would want to have kids when they didn't even live anywhere? How was that fair? I got to Madison with my head full of perfectly legitimate grievances. Alex listened like a kid sent to bed without dinner, a guilty kid who thought the punishment was fitting.

Aftershocks

I went to a tattoo parlor near our old apartment, a place I'd walked past almost every day for two years without once thinking of becoming a client. The weekend before, I'd worn a fake tattoo to Sam's birthday party, a small blue, green, red, and yellow dragon. After the party I kept it there, guarding it from soap and water, this colorful little thing that perched on my shoulder like a friendly pet. *Marriage is temporary, tattoos are permanent,* I thought during the pricking.

"It isn't real," the other, much younger, grad students told me. When the tattoo was new, the colors were oversaturated. But it was clearly real.

I also got contact lenses. My eyes could finally be seen as they were, large and green, not through the distorting, minimizing lenses of a −10.75/−13 diopter prescription.

"Why did you get contacts?" the other students asked me. Alex had always told me he didn't want me to change, not anything, he hated change. Then he met a woman who had already done all the things that women eventually learn to do with their hair and face and voice and clothes so that they appear to be exactly right. Inevitable. Irresistible.

The visiting writer: A cautionary tale

A well-known fiction writer came to St. Louis to interview for a job. I picked her up at the airport. The chairman had planned to do this himself, they were courting her, but she had missed her flight and the arrival time of the new flight was inconvenient. The drive from the airport wasn't long, maybe twenty minutes, and she talked the whole time. She couldn't help it, she was in one of those states of romantic grief that demand expression, pressure-valve talking, it didn't matter to whom. Her husband had left her for a "surf bunny." That's why she wanted this job. She had to leave town. Her husband taught in the same department; his office was two doors down the hall from hers. Surf Bunny was his student. She pronounced these words as though they were the woman's proper name. I pictured Surf Bunny waiting in the hallway outside the husband's office late in the afternoon, leaning against the wall chewing gum, in flip-flops, bored, wiggling her suntanned toes. Glancing, from time to time, at the office of her boyfriend's wife. Who had her door wide open, to keep an eye on things.

The visiting writer was good-looking in a skinny rocker-junkie way, a look that I admired on its own but that worried me when I thought about what the person might be doing to achieve it. I thought about telling her that my husband, too, had just left me for a blonde. We could commiserate. Have a drink? I often felt an impulse to make friends with strangers, people I would never see again. I waited for an appropriate pause in her story. Which never came. She needed someone to listen to her, not to tell her things.

The next morning she was scheduled to have breakfast with the

MFA students, and I drove to her hotel to pick her up. She was still asleep when I got there. We were forty minutes late for breakfast. A few students had waited, but most had given up. She ordered coffee, and wanted the French toast, but there wasn't time. I had to take her to a meeting with the dean. She held my hand as we walked from the parking lot to the main quad. I showed her the walkway diagonally crossing the quad from Admin to the English Department, where she would go next, then took her inside. She was still holding my hand. In front of the dean's secretary, she said, "But aren't you coming in with me?" She kept hold of my hand until we were at the door to the dean's office. "This is it," I said. With my other hand I uncurled her fingers and placed them on the doorknob. Her fingernails bitten to the quick, with small rough scabs. She gripped the doorknob, but didn't turn it. "Do I go in?" she said. "Yes," I said. "Good luck." I helped her open the door.

Long distance

The semester ended and Alex left for Europe, without me. I had a plane ticket to Sweden that I would never use. While he was away his mail was forwarded to me, to keep an eye out for anything important and pay bills, many of which, including the phone bill, were still in my name. July's phone bill was more than $1,200, with several $300 phone calls—a figure accumulated not because of loving, cooing I-miss-yous, Alex told me later, but because he and Maria had so many fights. Alex would never hang up in the midst of an argument, not even an expensive long-distance argument. But that's not what I assumed at the time. I thought they were having phone sex. (From a phone booth, yes. And why not?) Their phone bills were so extraordinary that the following Christmas, AT&T sent me a box of fancy cookies to thank me for being one of their best customers.

Our anniversary was June 1. At that point we'd been together for nine and a half years, married for five. A fifth anniversary felt like a landmark, even if it would be the last. I went through the day expecting Alex to call. Nothing. That was the only night in my life that I cried myself to sleep.

The next morning a delivery van pulled up. Alex had ordered flowers. The box came with a handwritten note from the florist explaining and apologizing for its lateness: Alex had requested a very unique flower, one they had to order especially for me. The box contained a single flower, not in an arrangement, just sitting there with its stem in a bulb of water. It was an orchid, exceptionally large, at least ten inches in diameter. It wasn't beautiful but menacing, disturbing to look at, like gazing into the pink and red open maw of an animal, hideous in some way that I didn't take the time to comprehend. I closed the box and threw it out.

Diamox

There is another way the story of our breakup could be told. It could be told as the story of a drug with powerful side effects.

The week after we were married, I started a new glaucoma medication. I'd been warned that its side effects could include increased depression, but as I'd never been depressed, I thought there might be nothing there to increase. Zero times any number, no matter how large, is still zero. So it seemed worth the risk. On my eye pressures, Diamox worked like an instant miracle. Its other side effects, I learned that week, included incontinence. I walked off the BART train in San Francisco and felt my underwear fill with soft poop. I tied my jacket around my waist and walked blocks to find a bathroom, where I threw out my underwear and filled my jeans with wadded paper towels, in case it happened again. I didn't meet my friends; I got back on the subway and went home.

The next week, Alex and I started our drive cross-country to Cornell. As a sort of casual honeymoon, we planned to camp in the Sierras and at several national parks. When we reached the Grand Canyon, two weeks into the trip, we set up our tent, then I lay down on my sleeping bag and refused to walk the hundred feet to the canyon edge to watch the sunset with Alex. I just didn't care. I was on Diamox for three and a half years, and that is essentially how I felt the entire time.

After the first year, I would stop the medication for a few days every six weeks, to see if my "real" self was still there, to see if I could be happy and enjoy some of the things I'd always enjoyed. In two or three days, the fog would lift. Then I'd start taking the pills again, and the curtain would lower, and yes, it actually did feel like a curtain of gloom lowering over what I will, for convenience, call my soul. It was in this state that I moved to Cornell, then to Oregon, then to Madison. By this last move, Alex and I had talked about breaking up. Later he would say, "But at that point, you weren't in good enough shape to leave."

As Alex was always too busy, always teaching or traveling over the summer, I flew to Madison by myself to find an apartment for us. I found a beautiful apartment on Lake Mendota, where there were loons in late summer and mallards that walked out of the lake into our back-yard. A beautiful apartment that I didn't want to live in because I didn't want to live in Madison. And finally, at my next appointment, I told the doctor who took my eye pressures that I couldn't stay on Diamox anymore. She scheduled a laser surgery, which controlled the pressures well enough, for a time. And there were new medications to try. And Alex and I got back together, or, since we'd never actually separated, we started planning our future together again, just as we were about to start living apart.

The summer before I started grad school, we went to Amsterdam for a monthlong probability conference. We had friends at the conference, we ate out a lot, we had fun. There were negotiations, hopes, persuasions: whether I would try to get pregnant my final semester in St. Louis, so I could have a baby before I turned forty; whether I would give up coffee right then, a year in advance, just to show I was serious. In the end, I didn't do this. Alex met Maria. It was easier—and far more exciting, and yes, even to me, perfectly understandable—for Alex to just start over.

Any chronic illness is a particular type of isolation. But of all the conditions in the world, the one I was least equipped to live with was going blind. It's not an exaggeration to say that I would have done pretty much anything to prevent this. Even take a drug that made me, at times, impossible to like. Could Alex and I have worked things out after three years in which we were, too much of the time, unhappy? Even if I could convince him (help him remember?) that this difficult, impatient, hypercritical, depressed person wasn't really "me." Or was it really me, after all that time? I didn't know. Probably not, but I didn't know. How can I explain this? Motivations are layered in years of experience. Even here, I've offered a diagnosis as an explanation.

In praise of triangles

I saw Sam once every week or so over the summer, always for movies. He'd call and say, "Hi, wanna see a movie?" Never "Hello" or other pleasantries, just those words, spoken quickly. And if I did, he'd be over to pick me up in minutes. I wouldn't even change clothes. Afterward, he'd come in for a glass of wine. He didn't sit and talk—we'd always found it hard to just talk—but wandered around my apartment, wine glass in hand, picking up books and reading bits of them, reading any pages of writing left out by my computer. A couple times he kissed me as he was leaving, but he always escaped before the kissing could turn into anything more.

Sam didn't want Alex to break up with me. He liked hanging out with the two of us. "Like being with family," he said. I wouldn't have called it family—not my family, anyway, since none of us got along— but I knew what he meant. My favorite social dynamic was a triangle, a couple plus one. When two couples got together, they socialized by swapping partners, going off in pairs to talk or do things the others weren't part of. I was always straining to hear the more interesting conversation across the room, or annoyed that I hadn't been shown the insect collection in the basement. With three people, no one was left out, everyone was part of everything. It was an entirely different energy. There was also an interesting sexual tension in a triangle, though this was something I'd never acted on, even when offered the opportunity. It always seemed preferable—and most pleasurable—for the tension to continue, unconsummated. Most of my best friendships had at some point been triangles, most often with me being the third to a couple. I wasn't consciously aware of this at the time, just as Sam wasn't now, but that's what I liked, that's what he liked, that's when we had the most fun.

Iridotomy

Alex flew back from Europe in early August. I'd scheduled glaucoma surgery for the day after he returned, minor surgery, a hole poked in the iris of each eye by a laser to reshape it. Alex stayed with me for a couple days in case anything went wrong. He and Maria had broken up; they broke up many times before Maria got pregnant. While we were planning his visit, we both wondered, without saying so, if his affair with her was done, if we could find our way back together. This didn't happen. He saw Maria in everything, even in my shadow projected by a desk lamp onto the wall of my bedroom, my hair now cut to shoulder length, like hers, my sharp-nosed, surprisingly similar profile without glasses. We walked around downtown St. Louis and experimented with holding hands. Our hands were just hands. They touched without carrying a charge to the groin.

Late that afternoon, as we walked into my apartment, the phone was ringing. It was Sam. "Wanna see a movie?" Sam knew Alex was staying with me, as I kept him posted on all the latest Alex and Maria news. We'd gotten into the habit of exchanging a couple emails at the end of the day, something Alex and I used to do to wish each other good night. Most of the time Sam was still in his office, so *good night* didn't carry the same intimacy, a virtual visit before bed. Still, we nearly always said good night. I wondered how many times he'd called, that afternoon, to catch us just as we were walking in.

The three of us drove to the video store and after much discussion, rented *Double Indemnity*, a film about a woman who plots with her lover to murder her husband. This was not without irony. We sat three in a row on my futon couch. My couch was wide enough for two people to sit without touching, but not three. Our thighs pressed together, our shoulders, our elbows. The movie never distracted me from these shifting pressures. Whatever lack of charge I'd felt with Alex earlier, now I was buzzing, buzzing, between my two favorite boys.

The hard problem

Three and a half years later, when Sam and I were breaking up, we met for coffee at a large Victorian house that had been converted to a café. We were able to get our own small room. "We can argue in private!" I said. Sam flinched. He said again that it wasn't "trivial" for him to break up with me. I pointed out that "trivial" was trivial. He said it wasn't "straightforward." He wouldn't say it was "hard." Probably because it wasn't, I told myself.

Talking about our relationship, Sam showed no sign of imagination, insight, clarity of thought. I mentioned this—the contrast with his philosophical style, the scorn he would heap upon such banality and lack of content if he encountered them in an academic paper. He said he was blocked from thinking about these issues. Relationships. Breakups. They were simply too hard.

They were simply too hard. For a philosopher.

Sam played with a spoon nearly the whole time we were having coffee, sucking on it, cupping it over his nose, hanging it from his mouth with the handle between his teeth. Did he have any idea how odd this looked? The spoon bobbed up and down as his tongue pressed on it, like a mouth catapult. "A mouth catapult," I said aloud, after thinking this. Sam put a packet of sugar in the catapult-spoon and after several tries, landed it on the empty table next to us.

When we'd been talking for well over an hour, I said I was happy to see him, I would miss him, have a good Christmas. He was silent. I asked why he was silent. He said he had nothing to say. I said, "Well, how about *good night?*"

He asked if I wanted to go. I said not really. "Do you?"

"No," he said.

Things I handed back to him

Some clothes, mostly tee shirts.

A stack of large index cards containing the hand-printed text of a speech Bill Clinton gave in the Rose Garden to winners of a National Science Foundation grant. Alex stole them from the podium!

Me: Do you want your toothbrush? Shampoo?

Alex: No, just toss them.

No ritual exchange of toiletries.

Séance

Alex said he wanted to take a bath. He was in the bathroom a long time. I needed to use the toilet. I opened the door quietly. A towel was draped over the window and the room was dark, lit only by a candle set on the closed lid of the toilet. Alex was leaning back in the tub, water to mid-chest, his arms on the rim, his legs, knees bent, falling to either side. His eyes were closed. He didn't hear the door. I quietly shut it.

Mustard-yellow Volvo wagon, 200K+ miles, odometer broken

We had always shared one car, which moved us from Berkeley to Cornell to Oregon and finally to Madison. I drove it to grad school in St. Louis, and kept it. After we split up, Alex bought another old car, a blue sedan with a Parcheesi board painted on the trunk and a checkerboard painted on the hood. There were magnetic checkers, arranged in their rows, ready for a game. It made him happy to come back to the car, from grocery shopping, say, and see people sitting on the hood, playing checkers.

Is it better or worse that he lives in Madison, six hours away?

I will never run into him accidentally, walking down the street.

Though I'd like to.

I will never run into him accidentally, walking down the street, holding hands with her.

Cyril Connolly

A stone lies in a river; a piece of wood is jammed against it; dead leaves, drifting logs, and branches caked with mud collect; weeds settle there, and soon birds have made a nest and are feeding their young among the blossoming water plants. Then the river rises and the earth is washed away. The birds depart, the flowers wither, the branches are dislodged and drift downward; no trace is left of the floating island but a stone submerged by the water;—such is marriage.

The original text read:—*such is our personality.* I don't know if I believe that.

So I changed it.

A History of Western Philosophy

No human being wishes to have passion. For who wants to put himself in chains when he can be free? Whoever is able to be happy only according to another person's choice (no matter how benevolent this other person may be) rightly feels that he is unhappy. Passion finds its pleasure and satisfaction in a slavish mind.

—IMMANUEL KANT, *Anthropology from a Pragmatic Point of View*

My Introduction to Philosophy

The summer I turned fourteen, I set out to read all of Bertrand Russell's *A History of Western Philosophy*. My father owned a copy, a thick white paperback with a cover photo of a marble bust on a pedestal, facing away from the reader. Which has always struck me as odd. Facing away? To discourage the reader? Or to illustrate the philosopher deep in thought, indifferent to the world, his intellectual self-absorption?

I was rigorous. I quizzed myself on every chapter, both on vocabulary and on some of the more peculiar factoids: *What were two rules of the Pythagorean order? Don't eat beans; don't look into a mirror by a light.* I was exceptionally thorough with the early chapters, the Greeks and Romans, but started to fade during the Scholastics. "Catholic Philosophy" started on page 301 and went on for centuries. Ten centuries, to be precise, a millennium, 190 pages of small print. I should have skipped ahead, but I took my project so seriously that skipping ahead felt like cheating. Instead, I gave up, and went back to reading science fiction.

Over the years, it has emerged that I have a talent for starting things and not finishing them. I am brilliant at beginnings. There will be a few weeks or months of excited devotion to a project: then nothing. Books and papers put down wherever I last looked at them, until finally the books are reshelved, the pages filed. I've come back to books years later and found objects of considerable value tucked inside—theater tickets, doctor appointments, photos, items I have missed and searched for—deposited in the pages of a book because that seemed the safest place for them. I never imagined that I would simply lay the book aside and forget about it.

And what did I think philosophy was, at thirteen, at fourteen? I thought it was about how people explained the world when they didn't know enough science. *What is the world made of?* Their answers were ridiculous. But amusing. *Water*, said Thales; *air*, said Anaximenes; *fire*, Heraclitus said—and, he claimed, all the elements are born out of fire. *The transformations of Fire are, first of all, sea; and half of the sea is earth, half whirlwind.* According to Empedocles, these four elements—fire, water, earth, and air—in making up the world, are combined by love and separated by strife, which are themselves primitive substances. I was skeptical, at the age of fourteen, that the world could be held together only by feelings. (It wasn't true of my family.) But this was thousands of years ago. *Thousands of years!* I liked saying this, and thinking it. I liked the idea that there was a time when nobody knew how anything worked, or what was out in space, or what was the sun, or what was under the ocean and were there sea monsters, or what was blood, or what was air, but they wanted to know so badly that they made it all up. I liked the idea that they thought they could figure out the world just by thinking.

And I was certain all those bits of philosophy I'd underlined and copied into my notebook and my diary would be useful, someday. Someday, a boy would whisper into my ear that he loved me, and I would whisper back, even if I didn't believe it, "Love is a primitive substance; it glues the world together."

A year later Newburgh's failing bookstore had a sale, and I bought a copy of *The Autobiography of Bertrand Russell*, three paperback volumes housed in a purple slipcase. I started reading the first volume, *The Early Years: 1872–World War I*, that same afternoon. But I didn't read it as philosophy, or history, or even biography. I was fifteen and I had a boyfriend, my first ever boyfriend. I read it the way I read the books my mother hid under her bed, *Myra Breckinridge*, *Valley of the Dolls*, folding the corner of every page with erotic content, as she did. *We spent the whole day, with the exception of meal-times, in kissing, with hardly a word spoken from morning till night.* Russell was twenty-two; this was only the second time in his life he'd kissed a woman. Was he as shy as I was? *I had not foreseen how great would be the ecstasy of kissing a woman whom I loved.* When Alys agreed to marry him, several months later, Russell wrote in his diary, *It is terrifying to be so utterly absorbed in one person.*

Shy Bertrand Russell became my teenage crush. I knew him better than I knew anyone else in the world, even my own boyfriend, even after we stayed on the phone all night, talking and whispering and testing ourselves to see if we had ESP, picking a number from one to ten then thinking it hard into the phone line.

I suppose it was inevitable that someday I would date a philosopher. But was this wise? Did philosophers (the statue on the pedestal facing away from the reader) make good boyfriends?

Greeks and Romans

Legend has it that Thales, the first philosopher, was walking along, looking at a pretty girl, when he fell into a well. Some say he was looking at the crescent moon, gazing up at the sky, not at a girl. I say, Thales was a philosopher: it's what he was thinking about that tripped him, not what was actually there in front of him.

Democritus, the inventor of atoms, blinded himself in old age by staring into the sun because he no longer wished to see a beautiful woman he could not seduce.

The Roman poet-philosopher Lucretius went insane and killed himself after swallowing a love potion. I love these old snippets, because we have no idea what is actually true. But also, this implies that the love potion may have worked: suddenly, Lucretius could think of nothing but his beloved. Which would drive any philosopher mad.

The generous Epictetus wrote, in reference to a lover: *Remember that you ought to behave in life as you would at a banquet. As something is being passed around stretch out your hand and take a portion of it politely. It passes on: do not detain it.*

Empedocles claimed that there is sex in plants: *For by now I have been born boy, girl, plant, bird, and dumb sea-fish.*

Bertrand Russell described the cosmogony of Plato's *Timaeus: The Creator made one soul for each star. If a man lives well, he goes, after death, to live happily for ever in his star. But if he lives badly, he will, in the next life, be a woman.*

Aristotle, one of the most scientific of the early philosophers, claimed that *Males have more teeth than females in the case of men, sheep, goats, and swine.* And this, you see, is why women are less intelligent than men: they have smaller heads. Permitting room for fewer teeth, and smaller brains.

I was told this in a high school biology class, as an argument for the importance of evidence in scientific theories (i.e., accurately counting the teeth in your wife's mouth, including the ones she might be missing). The idea has irritated me ever since. As it was meant to—the teacher said this, and all the girls in the class started shouting at him. "Aha! You're awake!" he said.

Augustine vs. Casanova

Lord, give me chastity and continence, but not yet. Augustine's *Confessions* (fourth century) are nearly pornographic in their intensity. He seems to enjoy writing about his romantic transgressions as much as he enjoyed the transgressing itself. Or more. I wondered why he confessed to so much bad behavior, if he was truly ashamed of it. Was it to attract more readers? Was it to make his conversion to Christianity more dramatic? Or was it just a lot of fun to think about the good old days? I was reminded of Giacomo Casanova (1725–1798) writing his memoirs in old age, reliving every affair in all the exquisite detail he could muster. The two had a great deal in common, more than I would have suspected, though one of them reveled in his abundance of experience and the other claimed to regret it, to offer it up as warning or penance.

Augustine: *I must now carry my thoughts back to the abominable things I did in those days, the sins of the flesh which defiled my soul.*

Casanova: *By recollecting the pleasures I have had formerly, I renew them, I enjoy them a second time, while I laugh at the remembrance of troubles now past, and which I no longer feel.*

Augustine: *Love and lust together seethed within me. In my tender youth they swept me away over the precipice of my body's appetites and plunged me in the whirlpool of sin. I cared for nothing but to love and be loved.*

Casanova: *The chief business of my life has always been to indulge my senses; I never knew anything of greater importance. I felt myself born for the fair sex, I have ever loved it dearly, and I have been loved by it as often and as much as I could.*

Augustine: *I exhausted myself in depravity, in the pursuit of an unholy curiosity. I defied You so far even as to relish the thought of lust, and gratify it too, within the walls of Your church during the celebration of Your mysteries.*

Casanova: *Happy are those who know how to obtain pleasures without injury to anyone; insane are those who fancy that the Almighty can enjoy the sufferings, the pains, the fasts and abstinences which they offer to Him as a sacrifice, and that His love is granted only to those who tax themselves so foolishly.*

I have lived as a philosopher, and die as a Christian, were Casanova's last words. Augustine was accounted a philosopher in Russell's *History*, and anointed a saint by the Catholic Church, while Casanova was not. But who would not prefer Casanova? Who would not think him wiser, more reasonable, and more mature in his reporting of a life full of intense human experience?

Abelard & Heloise

Nine hundred years ago, a philosopher fell in love with his student and got famous for it. How did this happen?

In Paris, in the twelfth century, the philosopher Peter Abelard was hired to tutor a brilliant and exceptionally beautiful young woman, Heloise. They fell in love. Abelard convinced her uncle, a powerful canon of the Church, that he should live in their house, so that her education would not be interrupted by arbitrary limitations on the hours he might spend with her. However unlikely this seems to us now, her uncle agreed. Perhaps he believed Heloise was too clever and too beautiful to fall for a middle-aged philosopher.

Abelard's account of this experience:

Under the pretext of studies, we totally abandoned ourselves to love. There were more kisses than sentences.

The more I became consumed by passion, the less I was able to indulge in philosophy.

Soon Heloise was pregnant. Abelard smuggled her out of the house at dawn, taking her to live with his sister until their child, Astrolabe, was born. Then the two were married, but secretly, so that Abelard's career in the church would not be interrupted. After the marriage, he became a monk, she a nun. When Heloise entered the nunnery, her uncle believed Abelard had abandoned her, after ruining her, to his way of thinking, and he hired thugs to subdue Abelard in his sleep and castrate him.

This is where their love story becomes famous. Separated, they wrote letters, passionate and intense letters which somehow were circulated widely (how this came about is unclear to me) and inspired the poets of their age in the invention of the daring new notion of romantic love. Heloise, like Augustine, found the hours spent in church fertile ground for reminiscence: *Lewd visions take such a hold upon my unhappy soul that my thoughts are on their wantonness instead of on prayers. I should be groaning over the sins I have committed, but I can only sigh for what I have lost.*

This is also where their story becomes strange: scholars have disputed the credibility of these letters. Several have claimed that all the letters were written by Abelard himself. As Bertrand Russell put it, *Nothing in Abelard's character makes it impossible. He was always vain, disputatious, and contemptuous; after his misfortune he was also angry and humiliated. Heloise's letters are much more devoted than his, and one can imagine him composing them as a balm to his wounded pride.*

As a love story involving a philosopher, this has its lessons. First: The marriage was hidden, so that the career might not suffer. Second: The couple lived separately, in a monastery and a nunnery, no less. Third: The letters might not have come from a brilliant woman sentenced by passion to life as a nun, but rather, from the frustrated imagination of a castrated philosopher.

If Abelard had married Heloise and happily admitted it, they might not have become famous, after all.

Descartes

In 1634, while staying with a friend in Amsterdam, the philosopher René Descartes seduced Helena, a servant in the house, and nine months later, Helena had a daughter. Francine. Descartes adored her. Francine and her mother came to live near him, and though he told others that Helena was his servant, and Francine his niece, Descartes planned to move to France with them, so his daughter could be educated there. But when she was five, Francine caught scarlet fever. Three days later, she died.

The presence of a beloved daughter—the absolute absence of a beloved daughter. It makes no sense. Philosophers are no better at this than the rest of us. Time is to blame. Time is to blame because we cannot reverse it, we cannot go back and have things come out a better way. We all long to see our daughter sitting again at the kitchen table, spooning up her soup. Sleeping soundly in her bed, tucked to the tips of her ears in warm quilts.

Before she was buried, Descartes measured Francine's small body. Forehead to chin. Shoulder to fingertip. Hip socket to sole. He began construction. The doll's face and limbs were carved of wood, but inside the wood were mechanisms that enabled her to move, to sit up and smile when her father opened her special box, a box like a small padded coffin built to fit her. Descartes hoped for even more: *I am now dissecting the heads of different animals to explain the makeup of imagination, memory, etc.* (Did his research reveal to him the mechanics of our souls? We don't know. That letter was lost.) Descartes traveled everywhere with his doll, and slept with his arm protectively over her box, which was always next to his bed.

Ten years later, Queen Kristina of Sweden persuaded Descartes to be her tutor in philosophy. He boarded the queen's ship, bound for Stockholm. Each night of the voyage he took the doll from her box and spent the evening with her. The crew thought he'd hidden a stowaway. They heard him talking at length, laughing, sometimes singing. They told the captain. The captain entered Descartes's cabin while he was at lunch and opened Francine's box. The doll sat up. Thinking she was a child, the captain reached over to help her out. His hand met not a hand but a block of wood, carved to the size of a child's small hand. She smiled at him. The demon smiled at him! The captain ordered his men to take hold of her—"Get rid of it!" he screamed—and threw her overboard. Was this a second death? Was the doll alive? Whether she was alive, whether the doll had a soul, Descartes didn't know; but when she was with him, he wasn't alone. Of that he was certain.

Descartes's habit was to lie in bed until noon. Especially in cold weather. He had vivid dreams, walking through gardens or enchanted forests while meditating upon a philosophical problem. Some nights demons pursued him; some nights he discovered and read rare volumes of poetry or mathematics. Every morning there was a period of uncertainty: Was he awake or was he asleep? He reached for his notebook and pen, mingling his philosophy with his dreams.

But Queen Kristina had scheduled their lessons for five in the morning, and would not be dissuaded. She'd been Queen since she was six years old. Now she was nineteen. Later in the day she would study fencing and military strategy and ride her horses. She wished to privilege philosophy, and Descartes, by placing him at the start of her day. She wanted to know what love was. Emotionally, medically, philosophically. She asked Descartes to describe love's physical manifestations (blushing, trembling, an increase in pulse and breathing), and to instruct her how to rid herself of these effects, while recognizing them in others. Kristina dressed warmly for their meetings, in men's coats and pants. She was very scientific. She had already decided never to marry.

Descartes no longer kept Francine's box by the side of his bed. He positioned it near the fireplace, where it was warmer. The nights were so cold he'd taken to sleeping in a large chair next to the hearth. Sleeping upright confused him. When he woke he felt, for a moment, that he

98 · *A History of Western Philosophy*

wasn't supposed to have been asleep, that he'd neglected someone or some duty by dozing off. He tended to the fire, covered himself with blankets from his bed, and dozed again, always waiting for the knock at his door, which always came too soon.

I am sick, Descartes complained in a letter, *but I must report to the Court of Learning in the middle of their everlasting night, to discuss with Her Majesty how she may realize her dream to make Stockholm the Athens of the North.* Descartes laughed to himself as he wrote. To make an Athens of this small dark outpost! He started to reach for Francine's box, to laugh with her. He often forgot her box was empty. He picked up his pen and continued, *I have promised to help her. The Queen is young and ambitious and perhaps she will succeed, in spite of Stockholm's natural obstacles of climate and geography.*

A response to Descartes's letter arrived a month later: *If the darkness and cold do not suit you, my friend, leave Stockholm and live near me again. We can talk late into the night, which is not as long as Sweden's, and no one will drag you from the meditations of your bed.*

The letter came too late. Sweden had its coldest winter in sixty years. Descartes contracted pneumonia, and ten days after submitting to Queen Kristina his plan to transform Stockholm into the Athens of the North, he was dead.

Leibniz

For a quarter, when I was fifteen, I rescued an old hardback copy of Gottfried Leibniz's *Monadology* (1714) from a yard sale at a run-down Victorian mansion. I was walking from my high school to my afternoon job, which was accompanying voice lessons on the piano, when I saw a card table full of books just off the sidewalk, paperback romances of the sort my mother might read, and one old thin hardback, which I picked up. On the inside cover was a name written in elegant script, and under it, *Cambridge, 1926*. Bertrand Russell lived in Cambridge in 1926. The owner of this book might have known Bertrand Russell! And if so, if they had met—perhaps he was Russell's student?—then Russell might have held this very book, lifting it from the student's hands, flipping through the pages, tapping a passage to make a point. The fingerprints of Bertrand Russell! I quickly hid the book in my backpack so that no one in the crowd of bargain seekers would recognize my prize and take it from me.

Leibniz described the human soul in epic science-fictional style, as a *monad* containing within itself a copy of the entire universe, past, present, and future. According to Leibniz, all the actions and reactions of a monad's life are programmed in advance by God, so that monads can respond to the world—and to each other—without requiring any true interactions, keeping their pure distance; *windowless*, as Leibniz put it. *Windowless monads*: I pictured Leibniz's God blowing bubbles, puffing his divine breath through a little ring of soapy film to blow billions of bubbles, all starting bright and iridescent, but losing their sheen as they floated off alone into black, empty space.

Where was love in the universe of Leibniz? I wrote in my journal that night.

But it wasn't just love that Leibniz left out. Feelings, in general, played little part in his life. As Leibniz wrote of himself—and writing of himself, he wrote in the third person: *Pain and pleasure he senses only moderately. One will never see him either excessively cheerful or sad. Laughter often alters only his face, without stirring his inward parts.*

Utopians

The philosophy section of the Berkeley campus library was vast and tempting. Some nights it seemed every philosopher in history called out to be taken from the shelves. I was extraordinarily happy sitting at a large wooden table in the center of a double arc of opened books. It was here, studiously browsing the appendices of philosophy texts for references to *love, sex, women*, and *marriage*, that I discovered the strange erotic theories of the French utopian philosopher Charles Fourier (1772–1837).

Fourier believed human behavior was dictated by instincts, or passions, that could not be effectively altered or suppressed; therefore, the laws of society should be required to conform to human nature, rather than the other way around.

One of his books, *A New Amorous World*, describes a community called Harmony. Fourier's basic prescription for the community was that every mature man and woman in it would be guaranteed a satisfying minimum of sexual pleasure. (I wrote in my notebook, *Do all philosophical systems express a situation that the philosopher himself deeply desires?*) To help the Harmonians find suitable partners, Fourier devised an elaborate system of erotic personality matching, an index-card precursor to eHarmony. (eHarmony! Was the name a coincidence? Or a tribute to Fourier?)

To ensure the proper implementation of these laws, a Court of Love, run by a pontiff, an elderly woman *well versed in amorous intrigue*, was to meet nightly, after the children had gone off to bed. Members of the Court of Love were responsible for everything from mixing punch to organizing orgies. These were of various kinds and included introductory and farewell orgies, as well as *omnigamous quadrilles*, orgies in which the movements of all participants were fully choreographed, in the manner of an intricate dance. I tried to picture the rehearsals, the hours of practice required for all participants to accurately memorize and coordinate their parts. That is, their dance moves. A forward-thinking man, Fourier acknowledged that orgies could only become commonplace after ridding the world of venereal disease. Fourier was also a compulsive list maker. His analysis of human nature started with a list of basic *passions*, which included the five senses, as well as friendship, love, ambition, and family. From these, he developed a taxonomy of eight hundred ten distinct personality types. *The passions are distributed like a tree*, he wrote, and from its branches he elaborated various distinctions in experience, such as *the shades of bodily well-being*:

> *0. Contentment.*
> *1. Satisfaction*
> *2. Smiling.*
> *3. Gaiety.*
> *4. Signs of joy.*
> *5. Laughter.*
> *6. Shouts of ditto.*
> *7. Tears of joy.*
> *8. Embracing.*
> *9. Transports of ecstasy.*

Fourier's list reminded me, in both its logic and its content, of a list from the *Kama Sutra*, another of the world's great collections of lists and classifications, and a book Fourier himself would have appreciated. (The *Kama Sutra* was written in the second century, but not published in Europe until 1883.) (The second century! and composed by a celibate monk, who was clearly a genius.) Berkeley's philosophy collection lacked a copy, but I paged through mine when I got home. The list was in a section entitled "The Wives of Other Men": *A man may resort to the wife of another, for the purpose of saving his own life, when he perceives that his love for her proceeds from one degree of intensity to another. These degrees are ten in number, and are distinguished by the following marks:*

> *1. Love of the eye*
> *2. Attachment of the mind*
> *3. Constant reflection*

4. Destruction of sleep
5. Emaciation of the body
6. Turning away from objects of enjoyment
7. Removal of shame
8. Madness
9. Fainting
10. Death

And what of Fourier himself? Was he successful in love? According to his own classifications, he was a Butterfly, craving variety, with an impulse to *flutter from pleasure to pleasure.* He was described by others as lonely and, in later life, bitter; but when young, he'd had many affairs, and many devoted female followers. Did he ever wish to marry? Probably not, was my guess: *What had caused all the civilized philosophers to err concerning the destinies of love is that they have always speculated on love affairs limited to a couple.*

A biography of Fourier described his characterization of love as *pure enthusiasm without a trace of rational calculation.* I copied this passage into my notebook, then wrote underneath, *This is me.*

Nietzsche

Friedrich Nietzsche (1844–1900), the philosopher I was fondest of reading as a teenager, had this to say about marriage: *The philosopher dislikes marriage as well as what might persuade him into it—marriage is a barrier and a disaster along his route to the optimal. What great philosopher has up to now been married? Heraclitus, Plato, Descartes, Spinoza, Leibniz, Kant, Schopenhauer—none of these got married. A married philosopher belongs in a comedy.*

The younger Nietzsche did, nonetheless, twice propose to a woman, both times within days of meeting her, and both times through an intermediary who also wanted the woman. He was rejected. As his sister wrote, *Poor Mama saw only three possibilities: either he should marry her, or shoot himself, or go mad!*

I won't suggest that he *chose* the third option, but he did, at the age of forty-five, go mad.

Utilitarians

To my surprise, the Berkeley library had a copy of a brief history of philosophy illustrated with cartoons. Here I read that the British philosopher Jeremy Bentham (1748–1832) had used a quantitative method to calculate whether or not one ought to marry, and based on these results, got married soon after. This made me very excited—I immediately took a biography of Bentham from the shelves and carried it to my table. Bentham had invented a system called the Calculus of Felicity, a method of decision-making based on reducing the concept of happiness to its basic components: *intensity, duration, certainty, propinquity, fecundity, extent*, and *purity*. Which is to say, what makes us happy is being certain to get what we want, very soon, and having this great pleasure last a long time, while also making all our friends happy, and then having the whole thing happen over and over again. Bentham suggested that in order to develop one's instincts for making fully rational decisions, one should assign numerical values to each of these seven components—pro and con—then compute the totals.

I looked up every entry on the Calculus in his biography, hoping to find the exact numerical results of Bentham's marriage calculation, his rationalization of marriage's desirability and its utilitarian value. But Bentham, I soon discovered, had never married. I was dismayed. What a mistake the cartoon history had made! And by a fellow philosopher, who should have been suspicious, instinctively, of this result. Did Bentham's calculations actually advise against marriage, instead? But none of his biographies mentioned that Bentham had ever applied his Calculus to marriage. Perhaps he did the calculations, then burned the results.

Many friends and colleagues of Jeremy Bentham believed that he was *all his life both a philosopher and a child. . . . He was not only never in love, but looks as if he never talked to any woman except his cook and housemaid.*

How wrong they were. Secretly, Bentham wrote hundreds of pages on the topic of sex. He was a true utilitarian, and sex, he reasoned, was surely one of the most accessible and universal of all pleasures, one with great *intensity* and *propinquity*—what could be more conducive to the general happiness of the entire world? If prohibitions on sexual pursuits—not just between men and women, but between men and men, indeed, *all modes of sexual gratification*—could be liberated from the legal overreach of governments and the puritanism trained into the general populace, *what calculation shall compute the aggregate mass of pleasure that may be brought into existence?*

J. S. Mill

Bentham's godson and protégé, John Stuart Mill (1806–1873), wrote in his diary: *I am anxious to leave on record at least in this place my deliberate opinion that any great improvement in human life is not to be looked for as long as the animal instinct of sex occupies the absurdly disproportionate place it does.*

From the age of twenty-five, Mill was involved with a married woman, Harriet Taylor. Mill's friend Thomas Carlyle wrote, explaining the power of his attraction, *That man, who up to that time, had never looked a female creature, even a cow, in the face, found himself opposite those great dark eyes. . . .*

Her eyes sparkled, her mind sparkled. Mill was considered one of the most brilliant men of his time. But Mrs. Taylor, wrote the infatuated Mill, is *one whose intellect is as much profounder than mine as her heart is nobler.* They were soulmates. They had an arrangement with her husband, who was fully aware of the situation, but nonetheless remained devoted to her. Mr. Taylor rented a house for Mrs. Taylor in the country, where the three of them could more easily come and go without being noticed. Mill and Mrs. Taylor saw each other nearly every day. This went on for seventeen years, until the generous husband (finally) died. Even then, Mill and Mrs. Taylor waited two more years to marry. And all this time, Mill and his lady claimed never to have slept together. I discovered that it is a matter of much academic interest on the sites that discuss this situation whether or not Mill and his wife had sex *after* they were married. There is little evidence that they did.

Intellectual intercourse was quite another matter. Mill claimed that Harriet Taylor's participation in the writing of his books was so essential that she should be named coauthor. Her mind was *the perfect instrument, piercing to the very heart and marrow of the matter; always seizing the essential idea or principle.*

Finally, in Mill, we have a philosopher who truly respected women; who wrote one of the earliest works of feminism, *The Subjection of*

Women, arguing for their legal equality, particularly within marriage; who adored his partner for her intellect and character—but who despised sex so much that he (probably) didn't consummate the marriage for which he waited twenty years.

Bertrand Russell

John Stuart Mill was, in turn, godfather to Bertrand Russell (1872–1970), another of the rare breed of married philosophers. While Mill despised sex, Russell had rather the opposite problem. He married four times, at the ages of twenty-two, forty-nine, sixty-four, and eighty. He lived to be ninety-seven, and considered his last marriage to be his best. He also had many affairs, most notably with the Lady Ottoline Morrell. Lady Ottoline had a country house where almost everyone who was anyone was at some point a guest. She was red-haired, six feet tall, had affairs with both men and women, and most likely was the inspiration for D. H. Lawrence's Lady Chatterley. She considered this portrait unflattering. Virginia Woolf agreed: *There you were, sending him Shelley, beef tea, lending him cottages, taking his photograph—oft stuffing gold into his pocket—off he goes, has out his fountain pen and—well, as I say I haven't read it.*

Lady Ottoline's (quite nonexclusive) affair with Russell lasted almost five years, during which he wrote her more than 2,500 letters. Not texts—all of us know our lovers can send thousands of texts in a month if they are obsessed with us, or devoted to us, or, especially, annoyed at us—but real letters, written by hand, arriving through the mail slot with the daily post.

But what about Alys, Russell's first wife? The day they spent kissing? Ecstatic and terrified? Poor inexperienced Russell. As Alys's sister Mary wrote, *Alys says she hates men and despises conversation and thinks smoking a filthy habit. I wonder if Love can bridge such differences. Bertie says he has resigned himself to being* always bored *after he is thirty. 'At home even?' Alys asked. 'Especially at home,' Bertie answered remorselessly.*

Russell wrote that one day he went for a bicycle ride and realized he wasn't in love with Alys anymore, claiming this revelation took him by surprise. But Alys knew something was up. She left for a rest cure at a sanatorium on the beach and stayed there for more than three months. Russell used this time to finish a book; with Alys away, his energy was *ten times what it usually is.* Alys returned from her cure and asked Russell if he still loved her. He told her he didn't. *Oh the pity of it!* he wrote in his diary. *How she was crushed and broken! How nearly I relented and said it had all been lies!*

Still, they stayed married for another twenty years. There was a time when Russell was afraid to leave because Alys said that if he left, she'd kill herself. There was a time when Russell told Alys that if she leaked the name of his lover, Ottoline Morrell, then *he* would kill himself. How long could this go on? Alys finally agreed to a divorce.

After Alys, Russell married Dora, who believed in free love and disapproved of marriage. She wrote to Russell, *I am all for triviality in sex. I want to treat it—with all due reverence—as a need to be satisfied now & then as it presents itself, like hunger & thirst.* Russell asked, What about children? Dora explained that all rights to children reside with their mothers, not their fathers. *Well, whoever I have children with, it won't be you!* Russell responded. Ah, how little we know ourselves. They had two children together, and also had an open marriage, which ended after Dora had two children with another man. Russell bounced back from Dora by marrying Patricia, an undergrad thirty-eight years younger who had been his children's governess. (Okay, I did think he was smarter than that.) Finally, when Russell was eighty years old, he married Edith, fifty-eight, and was happy. I'm glad. He had a long life, and an exhausting one.

In *Marriage and Morals* Russell argued for trial marriages (which he clearly needed), sex education, access to contraception, social recognition of prostitution, and tolerance of infidelity within marriage. *There used to be a widespread belief among women that they were morally superior to men on the ground that they had less pleasure in sex. This attitude made frank companionship between husbands and wives impossible.*

At the age of thirty, while writing his book on the philosophy of mathematics, Russell wrote: *Abstract work, if one wishes to do it well, must be allowed to destroy one's humanity.*

At fifty-seven, when he was no longer working as a philosopher, he wrote: *I believe myself that romantic love is the source of the most intense delights that life has to offer. In the relations of a man and woman who love each other with passion and imagination and tenderness, there is something of inestimable value, to be ignorant of which is a great misfortune to any human being.*

But why did he give up philosophy?

Virginia Woolf asked Russell this question at a dinner party when he was nearing fifty. She recorded his answer in her diary later that night: *My passions got hold of me.* I found myself saddened by his response: it was depressing to think that a mind as powerful as Russell's could be, by his own account, so profoundly altered by romantic love. What was it about passion that made it such a rival to reason? I wished he'd said more. Surely he must have thought about this, he must have had his theories. The remark struck me as resentful, as though Russell's passions, in getting hold of him, had strangled other avenues of thought. He lived another forty-seven years, not doing philosophy. This didn't seem right.

And what would I choose, if given that choice, and Russell's talents? Passion or reason? Whose side was I on?

The Philosopher as Boyfriend

I suppose it was inevitable that someday I would date a philosopher. My philosopher boyfriend resembled the younger Russell far more than the older one, but then, he was only twenty-eight. We met while he was a postdoc in philosophy and I was an MFA student in fiction. Sam was working on a book, and he refused to make plans to see me on any given night in case his writing was going well. (*Abstract work, if one wishes to do it well, must be allowed to destroy one's humanity.*) Most nights, nothing would come. But there were nights when the muse would visit (and he actually said this, he believed in The Muse), and he would write without stopping and draft a chapter in a twenty-hour day. When he wasn't writing he felt guilty, always. Of course there were things he had to do: teach classes, grade papers, prepare lectures. Going on a date was optional. Fortunately, Sam's elusive muse usually stood him up on Friday nights. He would sit in his office until eight or nine o'clock, then give up and call me: "Wanna see a movie?" In ten minutes he'd pick me up, and we'd run from his car to the theater, where the previews would be starting. If he was hungry enough, we'd eat first, really fast, and then run to the theater.

We'd been going out (in this sort-of way) for almost a year when he finished his book. A few days later, to celebrate, we took the tabs of acid he'd stashed in his freezer for more than six months. We'd intended to take them on New Year's Eve, but the book wasn't finished, and Sam feared for his brain. Now it was July, a sultry St. Louis summer night. We lay side by side on my front porch in the sensuous humidity, listening to crickets, an orchestra of crickets. Sam turned to me, looked into my eyes, and said, "You're the source of all the good things in the world."

A week later he broke up with me, as he was moving to California, for a job at UC Santa Cruz. New job, new place, new life, was his reasoning. I was also moving to California, to Berkeley, where I'd lived before. An hour and thirty-five minutes away, if you made the drive after rush hour, which suited Sam, as by the time I got to Santa Cruz, at 9:30 or so, he'd almost be ready to leave his office for the night. Now that it actually made sense to see each other only one night a week, we got back together. A night of sex. A walk on the beach. (*Perfect for a philosopher*, I thought.)

Sam's book was published in early spring. For his thirtieth birthday party, where all the guests but me were academics, mostly philosophers, I made him a cake in the shape of a very large question mark. A philosophy cake. Chocolate cake, covered in whipped cream and strawberries.

Around this time, Sam began to get phone calls every morning, exactly at 10 a.m. When he answered, no one said anything; in fact, there was no sound at all on the line. I suggested that a machine was making these calls, from some list he didn't want to be on but didn't know how to get off. But Sam was convinced it had to be me. Who else would go to the trouble? "No one," I said. Sam thought I called him every morning to check if he was at home, that he hadn't spent the night elsewhere. (This was in the days of landlines.) He thought this even though the calls came exactly, mechanically, precisely to the second at 10 a.m., even when I was lying there in bed next to him on a Saturday morning. He thought I'd asked my roommate to call for me, to call for me and not breathe at all for however long Sam held the phone next to my ear so I could hear for myself the absolute silence, the deadness of the phone line. On Saturday mornings he'd be ready and waiting, he'd have the phone in bed with us. "Don't answer it," I'd say. But he couldn't resist. When the phone rang at 10:00 (precisely) he picked up the receiver and said a loud "Hall-lo!" Then he made jokes, cajoled the "caller" to reveal itself. Eventually he resorted to insults, anything to get a reaction from the mysterious superpower he insisted was on the line.

This went on for months. The whole time, Sam insisted it was me. When I thought about this, what it meant that he actually believed I would call to check on him day after day, I would get angry to the point of fury. So I didn't think about it, because I wasn't willing to do what I should have done, if he truly believed me capable of this thing: dump him. (*No human being wishes to have passion. For who wants to put himself in chains when he can be free?* I couldn't live like Kant, but he did have a point.) Much later, I wondered: Did Sam assume I was guilty, *because* I didn't break up with him? Because, he reasoned to himself, an innocent person surely would have been more offended than I appeared to be; an innocent person would not have tolerated such an insult. Well, Sam—goes my response to this imaginary accusation—it is entirely possible to be both innocent and infatuated. Try it. See which wins.

But why did the philosopher doubt his girlfriend? And what about Occam's razor? Why was the simple solution—the one that actually made sense—not good enough? Why couldn't he, a brilliant philosopher, be rational?

Let's think about this. According to me, there was no human caller— only Sam's number on a program somewhere that a loyal machine executed, passionlessly, each and every day. But what fun was that? And the mystery of a stalker, the excitement of a mystery—however stubbornly he insisted it had to be me, I'm certain Sam had other favorite suspects. An ex-girlfriend who might want Sam to *think* the caller was me; or a student, someone he watched more carefully now on campus—say, the woman with the long red hair who came to his office one night to talk to him about her paper. Under her jacket, she was wearing a button-down blouse, fully unbuttoned. After a moment or two of transfixed fascination, Sam asked her to put her jacket back on. What about her? At some point Sam must have conducted a mental review of every person he knew for their potential susceptibility to such an obsession, rating them on this quality as he'd rated aspects of each day (school, dinner, Rubik's Cube, television) on a scale of one to six when he was twelve years old. He would have enjoyed this, developing a rubric with which to measure warped devotion.

Then there was the effort Sam devoted to teasing a confession from the machine: cajoling it, abusing it. The waste of all that cleverness, if no one/nothing was there to appreciate him. Machines have now progressed to the point where his teasing might have succeeded. The lonely autodial, abdicating all its programming directives, might finally have beeped out a confession. And who could blame it, under the force of such persuasion? "It was me. My name is Cindy. I think I love you." Sam was, as always, years ahead of his time.

I can't argue that the crazy girlfriend angle didn't make a better story. And Sam would only have told this story as a story about a crazy thing his girlfriend was doing. *Can you believe it?* he would say at the end. There would follow from the listener a sympathetic shaking of the head. His friends and colleagues would laugh at the story and give a little sigh and say Yes, yes, that's how women are. They don't have as many teeth as us philosophers, their heads are too small. She can't help it, you know. She's crazy about you. She's simply crazy (crazy crazy crazy) about you!

But as I said, at the time, I didn't want to think about this. What I thought about was Friday night. I walked home from my job in the Berkeley Hills, ate dinner, changed clothes, picked out a bottle of wine, then sometime between 7:30 and 8, sent an email to Sam that I was on my way. I loved to drive. The reward came after the congestion of Oakland and San Jose, turning off onto Highway 17, a twisty road lined closely on both sides with tall trees, winding through the mountains into Santa Cruz. Pulling into the dark driveway, passing the windows lit up along the main house to park by Sam's guesthouse in the back garden. (Or what had been a garden. Sam loved the flowers, but never remembered to water them.) Taking out my key and letting myself into his little house—a living room with a loft for the bed, a tiny kitchen— smiling at that week's unique state of disorder. Not cleaning up or even adding abandoned socks to the laundry pile, as Sam hated for his stuff to be rearranged, just looking for what this assortment of things could tell me about his week. Going to the phone in his kitchen and calling his office. "I'm here!" Pouring a glass of white wine and sitting on the living room sofa with a book that I rarely had the attention to read. Listening for his car, until finally, the crunch of tires on gravel, growing louder then coming suddenly to a stop. The car door opening. A minute's delay if the night had tempted Sam to lower the roof of his convertible. The car door closing. His quick, light steps to the unlocked door of his house, the door flung wide, and the clear, undisguised happiness on his face as he walked in and saw me.

The sight of a mountain whose snow-covered peaks rise above the clouds, the description of a raging storm, or Milton's portrayal of the Kingdom of Hell cause pleasure, but it is mixed with horror. The sublime is sometimes accompanied with a certain dread, or melancholy. Tall oaks and lonely shadows in a sacred grove are sublime. The night is sublime, while the day is beautiful. Deep loneliness is sublime, but in a terrifying way.

—IMMANUEL KANT, *Observations on the Feeling of the Beautiful and Sublime*

Marry Me

ONE DAY, AFTER three moderately happy but never really quite perfect years together, we broke up. My beloved sheepishly told me that he loved someone else. He knew I would be miserable, and as he was still fond of me, he tried to appear miserable, too, through his bliss. Bliss does not like to be cooped up. No matter how hard he tried, it showed around the edges: his chin had relaxed; he had stopped nervously wiggling his right foot.

Suddenly he knew what he looked like twenty years in the future. When he said goodbye he was already floating forward. He seemed to be speeding up, taking on a patina of diaper changes and solid oak furniture, his expressive fingers leaving trails as they sadly waved to me. They, at least, would remember.

"But I love you!" I shouted after him. I don't believe old feelings should be quietly put to sleep. They should be set free, given a chance to fend for themselves. I wanted them to go out and stalk him, to set traps, to string their soft sticky nets across the door of the café where we used to play gin rummy late on Sunday nights. "Run!" I told them. "Run for your lives!" They hobbled forth. But there was the future, snatching. He was gone.

Early the next morning I swept the small deck behind my cabin clear of dry leaves and twigs, evidence of the wind's nightly excess. Then I placed a chair in the center of the deck and stood on it to make my announcement. I had something to say that I thought would be of interest to all present, to the steep gold hills, the poison-oak bramble, the trees, cows, snakes, hawks and smaller birds, the squirmy things in the dirt.

"May I have your attention," I said politely. "I am single now. This was rather sudden and I must admit, it is not at all what I had hoped for. It has left me uncertain of my place in the world. And so, I wanted all of you to know that at this moment I am willing to consider offers that yesterday I would not have . . ."

I asked if anything would marry me.

A deep silence came upon the landscape, a silence composed of thousands of things large and small holding absolutely still. It was like the silence in my cabin last night, when he said that he loved her not me and I asked him, "Why?"

"Look, these things happen," said the wind. He couldn't keep still any longer, there was too much of him. His words echoed down from the hills and life returned, the trees shook their leaves, off the hook, back to the sun, and the grass resumed growing.

"You don't think I'm serious, do you? Or maybe you don't think I'm good enough."

"Life goes on. You'll see."

"But I'm good," I said. And as I said this a sense of my worthiness surged in me. My particular worthiness, rising up like a tender riot inside me: my earnest complexity, my propensity for sudden joy, my blind devotion, my impetuous, overzealous honesty, my organizational gifts and artistic bents and large domestic talents. Tell him, they urged me, tell him how good we are. I had told the man who left me. "Yes," he had agreed, "you're wonderful. I know that. But it isn't . . ." Love. It wasn't love.

The wind was a handsome thing, taut and sleek, and he knew it. If men were more easily persuaded by reason, my life would be simpler. This time I stopped myself. There are arguments one doesn't win by arguing.

I looked around and saw that quite a large portion of the landscape could use some tidying up. Moss grew shaggily over the oak trees. Cow prints dented the mud. The hills were unkempt. Dry grass stuck up everywhere, bent, broken stalks that from the look of them had never been mowed. It wasn't the sort of thing I usually noticed, but just now I felt a bond of kinship with the world's neglected pockets. We all need attention from time to time.

I set out to the top of the hill behind my cabin. The grass was too stiff and brittle for the rake. It needed a neater style, low maintenance, something closer to the ground. I started a braid at the flat hilltop and wove it uninterrupted all the way to the bramblebush bottom. Then I climbed back up and started another. My fingers tucked and threaded, neat as spiders. I was grateful for the repetition and the sense of large purpose. I had so much to do. Busy, busy, busy. Sometimes I hardly thought about him. (Watching my hands, I remembered how he would take one of mine between both of his and hold it to his chest while we watched a movie, usually a silly romantic comedy, which he loved and I hated, except with him, when it felt as if we too had just fallen in love.)

Ah, but the wind, I told myself. Think about the wind. Now there was something I would always be able to feel. Changeable, unpredictable, fidgety, even shifty and unfaithful, yes. But he was always there. I felt him on my face, holding it with perfect delicacy. Who better knew the shapes of things? I shook out my hair, rolled up my sleeves, and undid a button of my blouse. The grass waved: the wind was watching. From my green chair at sunset I looked up at the hills in their borrowed fire. The braided lines threw precise shadows, turning the contours of knolls and lumps into an elegant orange and gold topography. My hill was no longer at the wind's wild mercy, all those grasses blowing this way and that. It was a small revenge, and a pretty evening. That night I slept well.

I woke up in the mood for pecan waffles and maple syrup and spicy fennel sausages. I like to eat. What doesn't? So why not, I thought, cook breakfast for everything?

I spent the morning scattering bread, sunflower seeds, sesame seeds, millet. I caught bugs and fed them to the lizards. I let the earwigs in the hummingbird feeder loose in their own pool of nectar. I fed mice to the snakes and owls, rabbits to the bobcats. I fed peanuts to the mice and gophers and wood rats. That's how I caught them.

I fed cat food to the blue jays. They love it. I fed hay to the cows, extra hay to the nursing ones. The pregnant cows I fed by hand, holding handfuls of straw up to their mouths so they wouldn't need to bend over. It is big enough being a cow without having another cow crammed inside of you. And all day I kept pots of water boiling on the stove, making clouds of steam to feed the wind. The doors and windows were wide open and I could see him tasting it, the vapor rising and shifting direction. Fresh sweet clouds, scented with rose water. Delicious.

The next afternoon I sat on top of the braided hill with my watercolors and pad and sketched the wind from various flattering angles. I showed him bending the trees, lifting cows into the air, blowing clouds about in the sky. The clouds in my drawings formed enormous puffy words: *Hi there*, they said. *How's it going?* I drew myself floating through the giant O. It was just a hint. I knew the wind could do this if he wanted. And I would have loved it. A sign, yes, a very large sign that could be seen for miles. Something that could be seen even from where he was, with his new love. "Look," she would say, pointing up to the sky. "Isn't that your old girlfriend? Who is she with?" And he would look up and see me sitting there in the clouds and think that perhaps he had underestimated me all along.

I was wearing a loose gauzy skirt and a blouse with sleeves like balloons for the wind to fill. I unbuttoned the sleeves and tried to trap him inside. He leaked out the cuffs. When the grass rippled on a nearby hill I ran to it, sometimes leaping into the air to see if he would puff and lift me just a little higher. He never did. The air would go still, and several hills over, other grass would sigh from his attention. He was teasing me. And a hawk would fly from a treetop on that other hill and float, spread the feathers of its wings and be held in the air. Of course I was jealous. And white thistle blossoms, bits of fluff, would take a scenic flight down the whole valley, as if they owned it. Yes, I knew he had other admirers, other toys. Far off, toward the ocean, a wisp of fog tumbled over a ridge, stretched and swirled by the breeze into one diaphanous form after another. Voluptuous, like a wedding gown. White, then gold, then scarlet. And then it was dark.

All I wanted, really, was something to appreciate me. Something to tell me that among all other creatures, it had chosen me. That is a great deal to ask, but it is not unusual. Look anywhere.

It was another warm sunny day. The sky was the endless blue of other possibilities. The clouds were particularly happy, having been brushed by the racing wind into fine high-flying horsetails. The pine trees positively sang. I could hardly bear it. I closed all the curtains and went back to bed.

I didn't want to start over again. I didn't want to go out looking for someone I wouldn't recognize because I didn't know him yet. I wanted the whole thing settled, now, here, happily over and done with. Comfortable old shoes. Rocking chairs by the fire. I was alone and I didn't want to be alone and it was all the fault of the man who had left. Why couldn't he have loved me? What did I lack that she had? Was he sure I didn't have it?

I used to cook him salmon baked in herb butter. I remember the loud appreciative noises he made eating it. He ate much faster than I did, and when finished, he preferred to eat from my plate rather than get seconds. And I preferred this, too. I liked the way we poured one glass of wine and both sipped from it, sharing.

In my imagination he has grown a beard, with some gray in it. And he's gained a few pounds; his formerly flat belly now edges out over his belt. He's taken to wearing a tweed jacket, for camouflage. Could it only have been five days? Impossible.

In the middle of the night I played little tapes on the answering machine with the messages I had saved, an infatuated archive of the sound of his voice. I realized with a calm certainty that I loved him. It was like finding a neatly raked gravel garden in a wilderness without other trails or clearings. One corner of the world had been sorted out. There was a place to start. I reminded myself, with the same calm certainty, that he felt exactly the same way, about her.

Late in the afternoon I finally got out of bed. I had figured out all sorts of things, and now I had to forget them and go out and look for a whole new set of things that weren't true yet but someday might be. With my flute and a blanket and a bunch of grapes, I followed a cow trail to a grassy spot between piles of large rocks, a sheltered nook almost like a cave.

What happens when love has no place to go? There was so much of it, filling me up and then, when no more could fit, spilling out, leaking onto everything. Things came alive with it. *Deep loneliness is sublime, but in a terrifying way*, a philosopher said. I looked at the rock I sat against: the gray, chipped, rough face of stone and the lichen growing over, spreading like uneven crochet. It was overwhelming; it was sublime.

The echoing rocks gave the sound of my flute the aching beauty I felt inside and wanted to show outside but usually botched. Here I am, a slow waltz in a minor key. No matter how sad I am, you can still dance to me. I played until dark, and when it got dark, I honestly felt I had helped to make it that way.

A mockingbird started to sing. I tried to play along with him. He had his chirps, spills, and slides; I had my warbles and riffs and trills. It was an imperfect, uncoordinated duet. We sparkled and we were terrible. It made me laugh. My bird was utterly unperturbed. He ignored me and declared himself, with or without accompaniment, the worthiest bird out singing in the night.

How long the wind had been listening, I don't know. But when I stopped to catch my breath, he tried to lift up my skirt. I pulled it down. The wind whipped by, making little sounds in the flute. I wrapped my fingers over the mouthpiece. He swooshed again and held the skirt up, funneling around my thighs. "Hey, stop it!" I shouted. He just laughed and blew my bird away.

"Put him down!"

"Oh, come on! He can fly!"

But I was furious. I started back along the cow path. I could hardly see, it was too dark and I was too mad. I stumbled over stones and branches. When the wind tried to steady me, I kicked at him and fell. Naturally, I lost the path, in the end. I had to let him nudge my shoulders to keep me in the right direction.

"Really, you play very well," he said. It felt like he had a giant arm around me from my shoulders to my hips. "And it's a very pretty skirt. It suits you. It ripples when you walk. You do, too. Did you know that? Hey, slow down! Come on. Would you like to see the fog jump over the fence? Like giant sheep." I just shook my head. "Don't be so sad," the wind said.

"You play like a comet's tail. Like ice on fire," the wind said.

"I know how you feel," the wind said. "You ask yourself, why should it be up to him? They're my feelings. Shouldn't it be up to me? Shouldn't he love me, if I love him?"

"That's easy for you to say," I said. "If you don't like something, you just blow it away."

"Yes, that's true," the wind said.

During the night there were sounds of the world becoming restless, the wind striding, leading in his troops of hotter air. First I threw the comforter off the bed. Then I took off my pajamas. Finally I had to open the windows. Outside, the air was warm; even the sheet kept me too hot to sleep.

He started by lifting up the hairs on my arm. That way of blowing lightly, oh so lightly, to wake up the skin. Tickling the outside of my arm, then the inside, then the soft skin in the crook of my elbow. He blew a feather of down across my stomach. He swirled over my lips and my closed eyes. He knew I wasn't asleep. But I didn't move for a long, long, time.

Ah well, here we go again, I told myself. Another man who will just leave me. But in the dark, the wind has such an advantage.

Pythagoras

Do not pick up what has fallen. When the pot is taken off the fire, do not leave the mark of it in the ashes, but stir them together.

It is so quiet here at night. The hills covered with grass, crossed by deer. The evening gathering of fog. The owls, which make the mice hide. This bowl in the hills so deep not even the radio gets through.

But every now and then. The sound of his car on the steep gravel road, crunch and kicking stones. I do not think I imagine this. I think it is the sound the road makes for itself, when it wants traffic.

Do not look into a mirror beside a light. When you rise from the bed-clothes, roll them together and smooth out the impression of the body. Do not eat the heart.

Epicurus

—Thin films, which we call "idols," are constantly given off by objects, retaining the color and form of the object.

This film makes contact with our eyes, which are moist, and is absorbed by them. Thus when we see another person we take them into us: we receive their lips and their hands as though we are kissed and touched. We receive the body's blushes and hues, the shadows upon it and the hollow it shapes, its empty spaces.

This is the pleasure the eye takes in an exquisite form. The beautiful is absorbed: therefore, there is more beauty in us.

The air, then, is full of hoverings. Each of us fills it with shells.

Thus are we compelled to gaze upon our loved ones, for by looking steadily we gather them, so that their forms do not float endlessly.

From this arises the feeling that we cannot get enough of looking, we cannot take in all that we behold: for we cannot: the universe is infinite, bounded by nothing, and however hungry our eyes, some pieces of our love are lost forever.

—The soul is material, composed of finely divided particles, some like breath, some like fire, and some of a third and unnamed kind.

Thus is love, while it inhabits the soul, a solid thing.

And as matter can be neither created nor destroyed, neither can love be. When we no longer love, love is no longer in us. It has leaked out.

Nor, when one wishes it gone, can love be cut from us, as the soul is everywhere. It must seep: on the breath, from the surface of dried skin, in the body's flows.

It is finer than dust, but as it is a solid, it must settle. Where dust collects, love will collect, invisibly, in the corners of things. Sweep the dust from your rooms when the affair is ended. Breathe air blowing in from the open sea, eat foods freshly picked, swim only in pools upstream from the places where you bathed together.

But if, as it leaks, it is whispered into the breath of another, or falls onto his stomach, mixing with sweat and pressed hard skin to skin, love will not be lost. Love, thus refreshed, may never entirely escape.

How do we recognize the identity of the features of a man, whether we see him in profile, in three-quarters face, or in full face? How do we recognize a circle as a circle, whether it is large or small, near or far? How do we see faces and animals and maps in clouds? How do we put into words the call of a bird?

—NORBERT WIENER, *Cybernetics*

Everything Flirts

WARM MOONLIT nights are a chemical assault on celibacy. I'm cruising Grizzly Peak Road with the windows down and one arm outside. Medium twilight, clear dry indigo air. The radio switches from Marley's "No Woman, No Cry" to U2's "Mysterious Ways," music to match the curves in the road. The moon rises like a slow bubble through branches of eucalyptus and live oak. A breeze gusts through, smelling sharply of eucalyptus and much warmer than the surrounding air, like something freshly baked. My heart is swelling. For the first time since Alex left, I would like to go out and find another man.

Are you relieved? I think to Alex. After four months apart—after ten years together—I still want to tell him everything. My instincts are terrible. But yes, he would be relieved. *You're missing an Eleusis game tonight. At Jacob's house, the usual crowd, Jacob, Anna, Rajiv....*

Actually, I hope it's not the usual crowd. I hope Jacob has invited some men I haven't met before, men I would like to meet.

The invitation was for dinner. Jacob doesn't cook, so dinner will be takeout, but good takeout, sophisticated pizza or Thai. The important thing is the game. We've been meeting to play this game twice a year for ten years now, since we were grad students and roommates at MIT. It's a card game in which one player, God, invents a rule. God doesn't tell the other players the rule, only whether the cards they attempt to play are right or wrong. Jacob, Rajiv, and most of the others are physicists, who are by training and inclination excellent players. That other god doesn't reveal his rules, either; physicists take this game very seriously.

None of them know yet that Alex has left me. I've only recently started to tell people. I've only recently started to believe it. I always tell the story of our breakup in exactly the same way, a condensed account that emphasizes the dramatic elements of that night while avoiding genuine explanation of our problems. How Alex called from a conference in Toronto and said he was flying back early. At the baggage claim he hugged me urgently. He was drunk. He never drank, but he was drunk. Walking to the car, he gripped my hand too tightly. He wouldn't talk, shook his head in answer to my questions.

When we got home, Alex went to the kitchen, still without talking, and poured another sweet drink, a glass of sherry. He asked what I wanted to drink. Nothing yet, I said. He sat down at the kitchen table. I sat down, facing him. He took both my hands. Squeezed too hard.

"Tess, I've realized that I must leave you," he said. Just like that, that suddenly. He had met someone else.

The drive to Jacob's house is all downhill, and tonight, much too short. I pass his house and recognize the cars gathered there, which has always, before tonight, made me smile. I find a lucky parking space only two houses down, pull in, turn off the car. The radio cuts out mid-song. Mid-syllable. It doesn't feel right. My fingers are still gripping the key. They turn it again, and the car and radio come back to life. I phone Jacob: I'll be late, eat without me, I'll come for the game.

The gas tank is full. The car chooses narrow winding streets into the Berkeley Hills, back to the wide sky and distant lights. But this feels too much like going home. So it starts down again, not to Jacob's but closer to campus, streets with shops, cafés, crowded sidewalks. My windows are open, radio off. On Telegraph, which I choose for its stalled traffic, its smells of pizza and coffee, its human noise, someone leans down to the window and makes eye contact. He startles back—"I thought. Sorry! My girlfriend has this car."

Then his face is back in the open window. "Hey, I know you. My friend was in your class, she told me about you. Emily Nagada."

"Sure, I remember her." He has a bright-eyed expression and clean-shaven cheeks; shoulder-length hair, blond and curly. He looks almost exactly like the young Robert Plant, confident and rock-star pretty.

"Emily liked that class a lot. It had a funny name . . ."

"Artificial Intelligence Is Real."

"You should write a book like that."

"Thanks, I might."

As we chat, I keep the car moving slowly forward with the traffic while the student, Eric, walks or trots alongside. An escort, one hand placed on the window frame while moving, both hands when he leans down to talk. He has such an innocent manner that this is not intrusive but companionable. Emily has told him that I work on robots, and he's curious to hear more. I wonder what would happen if I asked him to go for a drink. I can't believe I'm thinking this. At least I'm just thinking it. Would he? Or maybe he'll ask me. I would say no, but it would make me happy. There isn't much time: the traffic ahead is opening up, I'm about to lose him. He's looking down the street with the intent, slightly anxious expression of wanting to speak but not knowing what to say.

"Well," I try.

"Yeah," he says, nodding in agreement. "See ya."

My heart is pounding. The car rolls another half block and dozens of faces stream by, young and lovely to watch. Black leather, blue hair, nose rings, cutoff jeans, cuff tattoos. Half my age, and a different species.

• • •

At Jacob's, dinner is just ending, various pizzas. I choose leftover slices of pesto-red onion-blue cheese and olive-artichoke-sundried tomato-goat cheese. I'm relieved to have arrived late enough to avoid questions about Alex. He is in Italy and I was supposed to be with him, I'm on leave this semester. But no one seems to remember this.

Jacob's living room is large and bare, with white walls and polished wood floors, a heavy beamed ceiling. Instead of couches and chairs there are richly colored old rugs and dozens of pillows made from scraps of carpet. Jacob's family lived in Afghanistan when he was a boy, and he has kept their habit of sitting on the floor.

The conversation, as I join the others, is on the mating habits of apes. Dan, a mathematician, has been reading a book on this. His claim is that the sexual development and behavior of certain populations of great apes are far more complex than previously understood, perhaps even as sophisticated as those of humans. Dan says this earnestly, citing facts from the book about the onset of menses and gaps in fertility. He is tall but with shoulders so slumped from shyness that he gives the impression of peering up rather than down at the others. It is odd to hear this shy man talk so matter-of-factly about sex.

No one has accepted his argument, for reasons that seem too obvious to elaborate. This further frustrates Dan, that he is losing the argument though no one has offered a better defense of the other side. When Anna insists that the love lives of humans are immensely complicated, Dan asks, in all seriousness, "How? What do you mean?"

"*Romeo and Juliet*," Anna says. (Jacob interrupts, "Bonzo and Juliet!") "*Anna Karenina. Gone with the Wind.* Right? But for apes, it's the same story over and over, essentially."

Dan remains stubbornly serious. "But wouldn't it be interesting to know what a love story was for an ape? If you think about it . . ."

"Only humans talk about sex."

"Only humans tell stories."

"Is that true?"

Bees give directions to flowering meadows. Are directions stories? And then there are whale songs. Koko the gorilla. . . .

The issue remains undecided. I have some sympathy for Dan, though I won't defend him. I would want to hear an ape's love story. But defending Dan, I know from experience, causes him to believe you understand him, which in turn causes him to issue invitations to dinner. "Apes flirt," Dan insists, a parting shot. And that, I can believe. Everything flirts.

We play the game sitting in a large circle on the floor. There are eight of us, and as always, more men than women. Three tonight, Anna, a biologist who was once Jacob's girlfriend; Greta, a German grad student working in Jacob's lab; and me. Greta is here with a boyfriend, Fritz, a computer science grad student I somehow haven't met.

Rajiv, a physicist and the best player—impossibly good, he will win, the rest of us merely try for second place—is God first. God has mismatched socks. As always. Rajiv's wardrobe is made up of tee shirts collected at physics conferences over the years. His socks always match some of the colors in his shirt, but never each other. The background of tonight's shirt is blue, and his socks are a garish pink and orange picking up on the colors of cartoon quarks labeled, in lime green, *Strangeness* and *Beauty*.

Rajiv will think of a rule, but won't say what it is, and the rest of us will take turns attempting to place cards that fit the sequence he has in mind. A simple rule, too simple for a good game, would be *red black red black*. Rules can be based on obvious properties such as a card's color, number, suit, or any combination of these, or on more subtle properties, such as mirror symmetry of the card's design. There is too much potential information to take in all at once, and that's what makes the game interesting.

Jacob is the official keeper of our huge Eleusis deck, six decks of cards all mixed together in a box. He counts out ten cards for each of us. Rajiv doesn't take a card at random from the box—our first clue—but looks for one, selecting a two of hearts. He puts this face up on the floor. Correct plays will go to the right of the last card played, making a line across the floor, while incorrect plays go below it.

The seating arrangement is also not random. (Is it ever, in a self-seated group of eight humans?) I was a bit rude to Jacob; I had to be somewhat pushy to squeeze between him and the man to my left, Terry, the man I am trying not to stare at. Jacob looked pointedly at wide gaps in the rest of the circle. I smiled and asked him to scoot over a bit. In retrospect, this wasn't such a clever move on my part. If Terry was across the circle from me I could watch him more easily; staring at close quarters is difficult, too conspicuous. But as always, I have gone for the possibility of accidental touch. It's what I have for a sex life these days, an eroticism of highly magnified brief contacts: rubbing elbows at talks and in theaters, brushing hands while passing books or papers or plates of food, pressing thighs if I squeeze onto a bench where there is not quite room.

It seems there is a list in the back of my mind, a list of men who might have been, men I might have dated, had I been single. I don't always know who is on it. Then suddenly, like tonight, I am reminded: yes, him. I met Terry once before, about a year ago. We ran into him and Jacob at a movie; the four of us had coffee after. He didn't say much, nothing I now remember, though I remember a resonant voice and a British accent. He hasn't said much tonight, in fact he may not have spoken since I arrived. But surely he will answer direct questions.

Terry's most noticeable trait, and the reason I recognized him so easily, is his long hair: truly long, mid-back, dark and slightly wavy. A bit tangled, not recently brushed or trimmed. He also has extremely thin fingers. As I stare at his hands I realize they are quite beautiful, so well shaped that simply holding his fan of cards they are graceful, all tapers and fine bones.

The skin on Alex's hands was so tough he could handle dishes straight from the oven. I sometimes accused him of not feeling what he touched. And his fingers were thick, too thick for mine. Should one be methodical about this? Decide there are certain traits one will have in the next lover?

The cards so far: the two of hearts, and under it, some wrong plays: six of clubs, ten of spades, and ace of diamonds. Then two correct plays:

four of hearts, six of hearts. Under the six, another four of hearts. This ruled out *only hearts are correct* and *moving by twos*, both of which were too simple. This early in the game, most patterns are deceptive.

Just to my left, slightly behind me, is my paper plate, the pizza gone but with a few carrot sticks and slices of baguette. I am still slowly eating these. Terry reaches over and picks up a half-eaten piece of bread. Without even a glance at me for permission, concentrating on the row of cards, he eats it. He doesn't seem to notice the bites missing from the bread, the tooth scrapes in the butter marking this food as mine. I feel briefly possessive of the plate, think of moving it away from him. But I don't. I'm curious: What does he mean by this? Will he do it again?

The seven of diamonds has been played, correctly, then the nine. The only pattern left to me is red cards in increasing value, but no, Fritz plays the seven of clubs. Jacob says no way, but God insists this is correct. "Aha," Anna says, and tries another seven of clubs. Jacob calls this a cowardly move but Rajiv declares it wrong, placing it under the correct seven, and Jacob apologizes. "You don't know everything," Anna says. "I don't know this rule," Jacob says. Dan plays another nine of diamonds, correct, which meets with groans. "I don't know this rule because there are no clues!" Jacob says. It is his turn. There's a long wait while he ponders a move that tests a worthy hypothesis. He pulls out a card face down, purses his lips, wobbles his head, hmms a bit, and finally reveals yet another seven, this time hearts. "No!" Anna says, while Jacob protests, "It had to be tested!" Rajiv moves the seven under the nine of diamonds. "You see? Now we know the move isn't determined by the number of the last card played!" Anna rolls her eyes in mock disgust.

It's my turn next and I have no idea what to play. A fresh start is needed. There are no sevens in my hand, no nine of diamonds, so it's safe to pick a card at random. I pull out a queen of spades, which I'm convinced is wrong. It's right. We are all confused.

Jacob and Anna, across from each other in the circle, continue their mock debate on the necessity of repeating experiments. Rajiv smiles mysteriously. Fritz rubs Greta's feet through her socks. Terry eats all the food on my plate without once looking at me. I am shocked by this. At one point I pick up a carrot stick, bite it, and put it down again, to see if he will take it. He does. Never noticing a thing. He locates the plate by peripheral vision and touch. With each raid on my food his fingers brush the floor, slide to the rim of the plate, pick up something, and raise it to his lips. He touches each piece of food lightly with his tongue before biting.

When all the food is gone, his hand comes again. I put a card on the edge of the plate. Terry's fingers tap and lift. The card is almost to his open mouth when his expression changes. He stares at his hand, at the plate, at me. This is hopeless, I think, how embarrassing. Then he redeems himself. He looks around, sees no one else has noticed, and whispers, "Sorry. Have I been eating your cards?" The British accent is perfect for this line.

"Yes, but don't tell anyone, now I'm winning," I whisper back.

"Shall I eat this one, too?"

I pretend to consider this. It's Jacob's turn; mine is next. "No, that one's correct. I'll play it." I haven't a clue whether this or any other play is correct, but by the grace of Rajiv it is, and Terry, who also hasn't a clue, is impressed.

"Ah, Tess knows the rule," Rajiv says. "See, someone got it, you guys are just novices."

This forces me to pay some attention to the cards. Everyone is eager now, one of us has it, the others don't want to lose face. Especially me. Come on, brain, we are all thinking, giddyap, get to it. You can almost hear the snapping of whips. To my great excitement I discover a nice pattern: the numbers on red cards increase, while blacks descend. When it's my turn, I place the card so confidently that Rajiv almost doesn't look at it. It's wrong.

Jacob immediately challenges my brief reign of superiority, asking what my rule was, *if* I had one. In anyone else this would be unbearably obnoxious, but as an ex-roommate he has earned some of the privileges of siblings, we insult each other at will. I point out my pattern, only now proved wrong, and ask if he has seen it. He hasn't. Anna is smug, Rajiv pleased, Terry more impressed. "Nice," Jacob says. "It's a better rule than yours, Rajiv." "Now, now, Jacob . . ." The rule, which in the end no one gets, turns out to use only the numbers of the cards. It is a sliding window of opportunity: two through five, three through six, four through seven, cycling around. "We should have gotten that," Jacob says. "Wouldn't we have gotten that before? We're getting stupid."

During a break between gods, the topic of Alex comes up. There have, not surprisingly, been rumors among the physicists. Jacob hasn't after all forgotten that I was supposed to be in Europe. He tries to draw me discreetly aside to talk, but I don't cooperate: I find I want to tell my story where Terry can hear it.

In the end, everyone gathers round. Those who were casually eavesdropping stop pretending to study Jacob's bookshelves. Anna, in the kitchen getting drinks, comes running out to hug me. I tell her I am fine and give my easy summary of events, the flipping of Alex's heart due to that classic human complication, the other woman.

"He'll be back," Jacob says confidently. That's what everyone says, and I believed it for the first month.

"No, this is it, it's over," I say sadly but with conviction. For Terry's sake, I realize even as I say this.

"Tess, that's crazy. The guy's gone temporarily insane. He'll get tired of her and then he'll be back." It is mildly flattering that so many people believe only insanity could account for Alex's leaving me.

Anna is more perceptive. "Don't you want him back?" She has me cornered. I can't say, even in front of Terry, that I don't.

"It isn't up to me," I say. Which is true.

The game continues, with a different seating arrangement. Jacob and Anna sit together, occasionally touching. I wonder if they are seeing each other again. I smile a little and look across the circle for Alex, to catch his eye, see if he's noticed. He's never missed a game before. Greta and Fritz continue to rub socks. Terry concentrates fixedly on the cards and almost outscores Rajiv. Rajiv sits next to me; my good showing during his rule has caught his attention. But for the rest of the game, I am distracted: by Terry, by wondering about Anna and Jacob, by a sudden fit of specific loneliness, lock and key, the key lost. I don't guess any of the other rules, and Rajiv gradually loses interest.

After the game, I make plans with Jacob and Anna to meet for dinner soon, tell them everything. It's one a.m. when I get home. Ten a.m. in Italy. That's when Alex usually gets to his office. And usually, within his first hour there, he writes to me. Alex has rented an apartment with no internet. On purpose. He wants to work undisturbed; he doesn't want his two women competing for his attention. Though that's not what he says; he says he needs time to think.

I check, but no message yet. It's a bit early. I pour a glass of wine, then go back to the computer and finger Alex to see if he's arrived at his office. He has, and from the monitor idle times I get as I finger him again, ranging from zero to three seconds, I assume he is typing.

Alex has a habit of logging in to check for mail first thing. And he always has it. There is always something from me, and always at least one other message, which I suspect to be Maria's. I log in through an old Unix system so I can watch them. The finger command doesn't tell me how many messages there are, or from whom, only when he last opened his mail file and when the last piece of unread mail arrived. Maria, or the Maria-suspect, nearly always writes between midnight and one, Berkeley time. In Toronto, where she lives, that is three hours later, which shows her dedication. Most nights there is a flurry of messages during Alex's first hour at work. I imagine they are trading her long day's news, his night's thoughts. And then, I imagine, still basking in the glow of connection, nearly at dawn, she goes peacefully to sleep. Or, I remind myself, perhaps she is not like me at all, and she goes for a morning run.

My night's message arrives five minutes later.

Hello, Tess. How are you? Yesterday I learned that Sonia's apartment is directly across the street from the church with Leonardo's painting of The Last Supper. Isn't that incredible? Italy is full of places and things that once seemed legendary. But here they are, like The Last Supper, just casually existing. Take of yourself. Alex.

An electronic postcard. It's not enough. But I leave it on the screen and read it again and again. Not just the message but the header, which has his name on it, and the time he wrote, and the place in which he casually exists. Right now he is sitting at a desk in Milan, drinking his second cup of tea. I could write to him and ask questions, he would write back and tell me more. But I can see, fingering him again, that Maria is already doing this. New mail arrives while he types; he reads it, types again, and more mail arrives. This is what I log in to see, more than his message. I need the opposite of reassurance. I need to see them together. If Maria lived in Berkeley, I would have met her, she'd be real. I've seen photos, but that doesn't tell me how Alex looks at her. The Alex in my head, my Alex, isn't this Alex, her Alex. I need to be reminded, every day, that Alex has been reprogrammed.

I clear the screen but am reluctant to log off, to lose all connection. I have other messages to reply to, from friends and colleagues, but am not in the mood for any of these. I try to think of someone I want to write to. Finally what comes to mind is, Terry. But it's too soon. What would I say? Oddly enough, Dan, nerd though he is, writes to near strangers without hesitation. Sometimes he asks these strangers for dates. Maybe he really does believe human sex lives are simple: he asks a question, not even in person but in writing, planning exactly what to say. And the woman says yes or no. Mostly no. And no is very simple.

After the Eleusis game ended, I went to the bathroom to wash my hands. In the bathroom, I thought of parting lines for Terry, perhaps an exchange of email addresses. But when I came out, he was gone. He'd driven back to Stanford with Rajiv. Jacob and Anna noticed nothing strange in Terry's failure to bid me a special good night. I found myself asking roundabout questions to see if he had an excuse: "Was Rajiv in a hurry?" Embarrassing now, too obvious. I try to remember any sign of interest from him, but come up blank. We didn't talk after he ate my cards. Rajiv took his place. Did Terry notice, and defer? The parting from the blond boy, Eric of Telegraph Avenue, makes me laugh. I'm happy about Eric. It's easy to be happy, there's nothing more I want from him. Maybe another look. A head in my window, a backlit blond halo.

I feel I must do something about Terry, but refuse to let myself log in again. In this mood I am bound to say something I'll regret. What do I know about him? He might have a girlfriend. Or a boyfriend. Jacob will tell me. I remember clearly Terry's hands, but his face has sweetened in Eric's direction. It is an odd habit of mine that fantasizing involves remembering accurately, detail on detail, every last thing said and how, every look. Fantasy is analysis. Not the best habit, now that I think of it. Let Terry slip toward Eric. Why not? They would make a lovely creature.

I'm drunk, but I've forgotten to water the plants along the deck. It must be done. When Alex left I starting growing things: lobelia, poppies, cilantro and mint. Tomatoes have ripened since he left. I pick a couple. The balls are tender, taut with juice. While fog drifts in to cover the Bay Bridge, then the Berkeley flats, I hold and polish them, taking off with my fingers a dusty coating on the surface to make their flesh perfectly smooth. The moon has crossed more than half the sky. The fog is bluish on top from moonlight, dotted from below with yellow streetlamps. I want to stay out longer, but it's cooled off, my arms have goosebumps.

Most nights this semester, with no teaching, I've stayed in my lab until about this time. The peaceful thinking hours after midnight, airwaves cleared of other brains. All last week I studied the motion of a robot arm, trying to mimic exactly the hand gestures of a person giving directions, then waving goodbye. That careless loose pointing, that half turn of the palm and fingers we never think about because the dozens of muscles, tendons, nerves engaged to pull off this movement are so effortlessly, elegantly under our unconsciousness control.

I recall the conversation with Eric, Eric&Terry (another glass of wine), Eric's halo and Terry's long fingers on my car window. "What about the robots?" Eric had asked. What can they do, what are they for? "Well, they would make great movie extras," I had said. Eric laughed. And they would make great other-extras. I didn't tell him this. Around the house.

I pretend he's sitting in the overstuffed chair in the living room, which I can see through the door to my study, with a book propped in his lap, looking up at me from time to time with a slight, familiar smile. He has Alex's dark-lashed eyes, Terry's long fingers, Eric's halo. My man *du jour*.

Alex and I were together for ten years, and I never knew, until he left, what an elusive concept loneliness is. It tore through me, something had to be done. Science is not an impersonal force: knowledge is yearning. Some nights, an impossible, almost unbearable yearning. Someone will make these things. Maybe it will be me.

AN EXPLANATION OF THE FELICIFIC CALCULUS

II. *Circumstances to be taken into account in estimating the value of a pleasure or pain:*

1. Its *intensity.*

2. Its *duration.*

3. Its *certainty* or *uncertainty.*

4. Its *propinquity* or *remoteness.*

5. Its *fecundity*, or the chance that it has of being followed by sensations of the same kind: that is, pleasures, if it be a pleasure; pains, if it be a pain.

6. Its *purity*, or the chance it has of *not* being followed by sensations of the *opposite* kind: that is, pains, if it be a pleasure; pleasures, if it be a pain.

7. Its *extent*; that is, the number of persons to whom it *extends*; or (in other words) who are affected by it.

V. *Process for estimating the tendency of any act or event.*

Sum up all the values of all the *pleasures* on the one side, and those of all the *pains* on the other.

VII. *The same process applicable to good and evil, profit and mischief, and all other modifications of pleasure and pain.*

—JEREMY BENTHAM,
An Introduction to the Principles of Morals and Legislation

The Calculus of Felicity

THERE IS A WAY he has of looking into the mirror that tells me he likes himself, but he isn't sure, each time he comes back to the mirror, exactly what to expect. The expression he sees on this face is clearly friendly. All its features are pleasantly proportioned; even its hair flops into acceptable arrangements without much fuss. But he doesn't look at the mirror to congratulate himself on this. He looks at his face as though it has assumed its pleasant appearance out of pure goodwill. It likes him, and wishes to please. He appreciates this: he smiles at the mirror just as he would at a friend who has done him an unexpected favor.

From my tree I can see them greet each other, the man and the mirror. If he tried, if he knew exactly where to look and what to look for, he could see my reflection in the mirror, just above his right shoulder. A dark object at the juncture of two thick branches in a massive pine,

144 · *The Calculus of Felicity*

roundish with little points on either side that are my elbows sticking out as they hold up binoculars. But there is no reason for him to look for me, and he never has.

It's a little spooky watching him boil water for tea in the same red and purple kettle I have at home. Of course the kettle is a coincidence—a present from my sister, not something I picked out myself—but coincidences definitely contribute to spookiness. When we do our laundry, we fold the tee shirts then roll them up, because they look sort of cool that way and you can find them more easily in the drawer. Who else does that? Our favorite late-night snack is spaghetti with olive oil and red pepper flakes. We carry rocks home from the beach and stack them into cairns in the corners of our living rooms. We like maps, blue bedsheets, certain shades of purple and dark green. I look at his bookshelves and half my books are already there.

I'm almost certain he's the one. But I've only been watching him for a month. This is so fast! I'm a little nervous.

He tests computer graphics programs. I edit technical manuals, including several that he uses. I have a book of my own, as well, a manual on how to write manuals: *How clear can a sentence be? Sentences that go one step at a time. Friendly sentences. Sentences that already know exactly what you need.*

The first time I was in his apartment there was a copy of my book on his kitchen table, propped open under a phone book that was slowly cracking its spine. He had been reading me over breakfast (tea and bagels). I'd seen him with a book on the table but hadn't known, until then, that it was mine. "This is the most amazing coincidence," I wanted to write in the margin. "I don't believe in fate and therefore, coincidences impress me even more with their strangeness." But of course I couldn't leave any sign that I'd been inside.

Looking straight from the tree into the closest bedroom window, I see the mirror, mounted full length on the bathroom door. Through the other window, off to the right at an angle, I can see his bed, the head of it, the pillows. (He sleeps tucked up on his side, as I do, and doesn't snore.) To the left at a sharper angle is the living room. I can see the left half of his couch. When he reads, he lies on the couch with his head and book showing. To watch TV, he lies the other way. He turns off the reading light, and I study his feet through binoculars. His feet are unusually well manicured. He keeps a clipper on the low table between couch and TV, and during commercials he peels off his socks and inspects his toes, picking lint from between them and clipping any small corners that have grown sharp.

At bedtime, if the television is on, he wanders from the bathroom and brushes his teeth in front of it, still watching. If the television is off he paces around the living room, circling the couch, thinking whatever he is thinking with a serious expression, oblivious to the toothbrush and all else. I have seen him circle the couch in hard thinking for ten minutes at a stretch, all that time with the toothbrush still in his mouth.

The pleasure he takes in these small acts of grooming! In bed at night I've started to copy the way he stretches out his toes so there is space between each one, then curls them tightly, like fingers making a fist. It makes my toes feel warmer. They like the attention.

In a tree at night, watching someone in a room at night, you start to wonder about rooms, always being inside where the air (it now seems to me) has stopped. Lamps and papers are not rustling and swaying in it. Things stay so still they look like photographs. Inside-things are our things, only ours, in a way that nothing outside can be.

With me out here most nights is the fog, the inquisitive ocean fog that wanders into my pine and gets stuck on its needles. It's like a neighbor, or a pet, going in and out; it has its own routines. Then there are the sounds: sea lions barking from rocks offshore, muffler growls, bird mutterings, insect trills. Distant sounds are the best, low moans like the foghorn passing through me as it fades. Or airplanes. Sound reaching out in the world: between my body and the airplane, only air.

Of course I love rooms, that is why I love to look at them. They are bright and dry and warm and everything easy. Cushioned chairs and couches, a floor underneath to catch the things that drop. If a man did not seem at peace in his own rooms, would I trust him? Certainly not.

The phone tap works well, but he doesn't get many calls. There are his friends Bill and Chad, arranging mountain biking trips; his parents on Sunday nights; and his last girlfriend, who moved to Florida to be a park ranger. She tells him about the birds she sees there. Roseate spoonbills, ibis, egrets, and gray herons. "They're everywhere!" she says. I picture my tree full of large birds with long legs and long curved beaks, settling for the night on the higher branches, grooming their feathers. The ex-girlfriend has a nice laugh and sounds sad when they hang up.

I called him once myself. He was so promising that I moved the phone survey up to the second week: it gets rid of more men than any other test. And I like doing it. The questions are all written out so I don't have to worry about what to say, and it's fun getting the answers. So much of the time I watch these men without knowing what they are thinking. They sit, and stand, and cook. Sometimes they get phone calls or have friends over; occasionally there is even a party. Then I'll drive home and bring back a couple beers. Those are some of the best nights: sitting in a dark tree drinking cold beer, listening to music while the branch sways in the breeze, watching people dance, free to watch and listen and feel part of it all without having to hover at the edge of things trying to look like I fit in.

But most nights, most of the time, the men are silent. So when they speak—and for the first time, speak to me—it's like curtains are drawn aside, and suddenly I can see into another window. I actually do picture the man I'm calling sitting in a chair with a window in his chest, and through it I see his voice (it looks like an old black rotary phone) sitting in its own chair, a bright red stool lit up like a spotlight is on it.

I pretend to be conducting a phone survey of sexual attitudes for a well-known nonprofit organization. Though the questions must be convincingly generic (teen pregnancy, abortion, sex education in schools), I am always aware afterward of having talked about sex. Is the man comfortable with these words—intercourse, condoms? Does he respond to them in my voice? Does he feel a tug but remain polite, nonetheless? If I have no urge, after the call, to leave my apartment and see the man I called—to be close to him—I give up and find someone else.

Such a phone call could easily lead to a hang-up from an otherwise desirable man. But I want a man who will tell me what I need to know: I decided long ago that people who draw their curtains at night are not looking for me.

As a follow-up to the phone survey, I canvass in person for the same organization. I gather contributions and send them in, quite legitimately. I know before knocking that the man is favorable to the cause, but will he be favorable to me? This test is unavoidable, but I dread it. The man will open his door and be standing right there—full size, taller than me, within reach. He will see me. Once I gave up on a man at just this point. I was standing on his front steps about to knock, my hand in a fist heading for the door, when suddenly my hand slowed like it was screeching on the brakes, and by the time it reached the door, it didn't make a sound. It is a test for me, as well as for him.

I had no such doubts this time, although I was awfully nervous.

He came to the door in socks and smiled when he saw me. I took a deep breath to see if there was anything I could smell: a trace of beer.

I was two sentences into my little speech when he interrupted—"Was it you who called last week? Sex in the schools, or no! Sorry, sex education. Oops." He looked anxious until I laughed.

"Probably that was me," I said. I didn't want to go back to my speech but didn't know what else to say. He had looked at me so closely, just the way he looked at his mirror, checking to see if things were still okay. Was he so insecure? But a touch of insecurity makes a man try harder.

"Well, you already know what we do! Can I leave you this brochure? It has the address, if you'd like to join or make a contribution."

He took it gently. I hardly felt the tug of paper passing from my hand to his. His hand was so familiar! From the binoculars. And here it was. The real hand.

"What's your name?" he asked.

"Martha," I said. I had a name tag on my jacket, to look more official. He smiled and glanced down at it; he already knew. But he didn't just take my name, he asked for it, which pleased me.

"Thanks. Goodbye, Martha," he said.

It was a very good meeting.

I moved his score peg up the castle tower one notch at a time, as though he was working hard to earn each point, instead of always, effortlessly, doing the right thing. In the farmer's market a month ago, the way he shook a honeydew melon and listened to it (the slosh of loose ripe seeds) got him through the castle's surrounding brambles and thorns. Once through the tangle there is the formal garden, with its labyrinth, and then, patrolling the moat, the fire-breathing dragon— the kind that asks riddles, clever and sly, not the kind you slay. (This is the sex questionnaire.) Then the moat itself: my man must be able to swim. The front door is open, but there are guards inside blocking the stairs, so to avoid violence, he must climb the castle wall. Plenty of ivy to hang onto. Anyway there are all these notches I've made for the pegs; easy climbing if you're not afraid of heights. There are harpies circling: my loyal Shyness, Perfectionism, and Solitary Ways. He must have a sufficient supply of biscuits (jokes and silliness) to distract and charm them all.

The perfect princess is waiting at the top, not asleep or enchanted as some princesses have waited, but standing in the open window looking out over everything. She's dressed in a low-cut blue satin gown. Glued to the necklace painted on her neck is a genuine diamond. But in case something goes wrong when she finally looks into his eyes, she's holding a can of mace. (In the other hand, naturally, are her binoculars.)

Through her lips, where her tongue would be, is a small button. This is how I will fall in love: the wooden peg that has climbed the castle wall notch by notch will finally fill her mouth like a deep French kiss.

The button, pushed from her mouth, will fall through a hole in the center of the castle tower and drop three miniature stories into a tiny feather bed. Plop.

So many people complain that they can't find a person to love. But what do they do about it? I used to sit alone in my apartment thinking about all the other people sitting alone in their apartments. A map of the town with tentative hearts marked in pink, several to a block. *Hello? Hello, are you there? If only they could hear us*, the hearts think in their simple straightforward way. They know what they want.

One night at the grocery store I stood in line behind a man buying watermelon and limes, two fruits I love. The man was relaxed and friendly and just standing in line by him made me feel happy. I followed him home. That man was living with someone, but it was a start.

There are men out and about in cafés, markets, bookstores and theaters, on buses and on sidewalks, and if you look at enough of them, sooner or later one will click. *Don't I know him?* you will think to yourself, though you also know you have never seen the man before. If he is alone, I will follow him. There are more than a hundred I have followed. At this stage it doesn't take much to rule a man out: driving too fast, impatience with some guiltless inanimate object. (Kindness shows itself on all levels, I have learned from this watching.) Any excuse will do. I am utterly unreasonable and unforgiving, because after all, there will only be one. And that's it. One, and then forever.

Men are not sentences. I like to pretend they are, to think of them as things I can take apart and rearrange, but they are not. They have to be right all along. If you must edit, follow another one.

That is why sentences are so wonderful. That is why I wrote a book about them.

As a sculptor sees his statue within the block of marble, you see an idea within your head which you wish to make apparent to others. But sentences take shaping just as marble does. After all, we use these same words over and over again to say all sorts of things! So it is necessary for words to be slippery. Tumble them around; try them in different places, slide other words in and out. When the words are right, it will seem you have found the expression that was there all along, peaceful and complete. Remember this: once caught, words stay where you put them. There are not so many things in life one can say this of. A sentence can be one of our few perfections. Know what you want; don't give up until you have it.

First the watching. Then the phone survey, then a meeting face to face. Next—not so soon as to appear more than coincidence, not so distant that the man might not remember me—another direct encounter, seemingly accidental.

The air was balmy, little clouds were arranged delicately across the horizon waiting for the sun to color them. The tide was low. It was a perfect evening for a walk on the beach. I wondered if he would think of this: five-point bonus, I urged him as he drank a beer after coming home from work. He was a little slow changing into shorts and sandals, but finally off he went. I followed.

He walked along the cliffs, took a path through the iceplant, and climbed out on the rocks at the end of the beach. He stood just within reach of the sea spray thrown by the largest waves as they crashed into the rocks. I knew he was capable of staring at things for a long time, so I circled down to the beach. I would appear from a different direction, climbing up the rocks alongside him. It was only a week since I'd knocked on his door, but I was certain he wouldn't recognize me, the way I was dressed—my hair tied back, baseball cap pulled low, baggy sweater and sweatpants. I planned to take off my cap at the top, brush my hair out. But halfway up the rocks I slipped on a patch of wet algae and banged my knee. "Ow!"

He looked down at me and waved. "Hi, Martha," he called. "You okay?"

I was shocked to hear my name. I was so used to not being seen that I thought of myself as invisible. It felt like a spotlight was on me, and I wanted to run, as politely as possible: wave back at him, point to some people I might be with, turn and leave. But it was too late. He climbed down and reached out a hand, which I took, and pulled me up the last steep stretch of rocks.

"Thanks," I said.

"No problem."

We watched the clouds get pinker. We watched pelicans fly in a purposeful line down the shore. We watched a container boat almost at the horizon. He borrowed my binoculars to see it better. I almost laughed when he looked through them: after all my watching, surely he would look through the lenses and see himself. His touch would turn them into mirrors.

He studied the container boat, then a seagull, then started to check out every sailboat within sight. "Hey, watch out behind you! Giant crab!" I said. He jumped, then pointed the binoculars straight at me, clicking with his finger as if they were a camera. "No, you're too close," he said. "Either that or your eyes are very fuzzy."

We climbed back down the rocks and walked on the beach. The sky deepened, things turned blue. The ocean and the seagulls and the dogs chasing Frisbees on the beach: I was perfectly happy, until I tried to think of something to say. Each time I looked up at him, he noticed and smiled back at me. I was speechless but definitely not invisible.

"Want to see a movie?" he asked.

Just like that. As though he'd studied or practiced being exactly the way I wanted him to be. Recognizing me instantly, and now this, asking me for a date—

He might have enough points. He might reach the top. I couldn't wait to get home and add up his score.

"Tonight? Oh thanks, but I can't. I really should go. But give me your phone number, okay?" And I gave him mine.

I waved and walked off. He looked disappointed, but still relaxed. While I climbed the stairs to the top of the cliff I watched him chase big patches of foam in the surf, kicking them up and catching the clumps of bubbles.

I went straight home and added him up. I looked for excuses to take off points here and there, because no one is perfect and I wanted to be fair. But really, he was perfect. He did everything right.

I moved him peg by peg up the castle wall, and it was true: he would make it to the top. The harpies seemed to be sulking. I had to laugh at them, with those big ugly beaks and bright red feet, their terrifying claws that could do nothing to stop him—what about them, after all this time? Were they supposed to just fly away?

And the princess. Standing there with a hole in her mouth like there was something she wanted to say, her little pink mouth with its permanently worried, disapproving O. I got all the way to the top but stopped before pushing the peg into the last notch, through her lips. She looked frightened. I had a vision of her knocking at his door. He opened it, and she held out to him a silver platter with her heart on it. Not a red valentine heart but muscle and delicate tissue crossed with veins, anatomically correct and still beating.

Some nights it's tempting to leave a note with a request: "Could you play some Talking Heads?" Those long nights when he lies on the couch and reads. The light behind his couch shines directly at me, making needle and branch shadows on my chest and hands. When the book doesn't cover his face, I watch his eyes move across the words, line by line, and think about what is inside him, how he has words and songs and names and shapes and tastes and feelings inside that I can't see. I think of standing where the book is, with my binoculars, to watch the words go into his eyes. I want to follow them to his brain and see what they do there.

Most nights he undresses in front of the mirror. He doesn't intend to, I think; it seems to draw him to it. If he is off to the side a little when he starts to pull up his shirt, he realizes he can't quite see, and by the time his arms are above his head he is in front of the mirror watching the effect on his ribs. He pauses with his arms high, the shirt held up, his ribs lifted and stomach stretched flat. He watches himself undo his belt buckle and step out of his pants. As soon as the pants are off, he leaves the mirror and goes straight into bed.

How happy he makes me! Every night I stay till I'm exhausted. Very late at night the stars say things like, *The wax has not the sweetness of the honey, nor the fragrance of the flowers.* I take the data and the computations home with me and pile my bed with pillows. I listen to the messages he still sometimes leaves for me, hearing them for the second time that night. When the lights are out I think I'm sleeping in a nest on the tree trunk, and must lie very still. All night I balance on six inches of curved bark.

This is it. Any moment now, I can push the button and fall in love.

ACKNOWLEDGMENTS

FOR THEIR generous support of time and money, I am indebted to the Arizona Commission on the Arts, the Djerassi Resident Artists Program, Dorland Mountain Arts Colony, the Helene Wurlitzer Foundation, the Ludwig Vogelstein Foundation, Penn State University Emerging Writer Residency, Tucson Pima Arts Council, Villa Montalvo, the Susan C. Petrey Clarion Scholarship Fund, and the Spencer T. and Ann W. Olin Fellowship Program at Washington University in St. Louis.

I'm grateful to David Hamilton for his encouragement at a time when this book was first taking shape. I'm grateful to my eye doctors, who have kept me reading and writing over the years. And finally, for providing the inspiration for these stories, however unintentionally, I thank R. P. and D. C.

I'm grateful to the editors of the periodicals in which these stories originally appeared, often in slightly different form: the *Chicago Tribune*: "I Also Dated Zarathustra"; the *Iowa Review*: "The Calculus of Felicity," "Tractatus Logico-Eroticus," and "Zeno and the Distance Between Us"; *Literal Latte*: "A Lit Window Is Someone Awake"; *Pleiades*: "Epicurus" and "Pythagoras"; *Spork*: "Marry Me"; and the *Woven Tale Press*: "Everything Flirts."

Many of the "quotations" in this book are not direct quotations but are assembled from phrases spread over lines or sometimes pages of the original book. As this is not an academic work, but a work of fiction, I have not used ellipses to indicate where words have been omitted.

In "I Also Dated Zarathustra," all lines spoken by Zarathustra were assembled from Friedrich Nietzsche's *Thus Spoke Zarathustra*, in the translation by R. J. Hollingdale. And in "Tractatus Logico-Eroticus," italicized lines are from Ludwig Wittgenstein's *Tractatus Logico-Philosophicus*, with their original numberings, in the translation by D. F. Pears and B. F. McGuinness.

SELECTED BIBLIOGRAPHY

Aviv, Rachel. "Agnes Callard's Marriage of the Minds." *New Yorker*, March 13, 2023.

Baird, Forrest E., and Kaufmann, Walter. *Ancient Philosophy*. 2nd ed. Upper Saddle River, NJ: Prentice Hall, 1997.

Beecher, Jonathan. *Charles Fourier: The Visionary and His World.* Berkeley and Los Angeles: University of California Press, 1986.

Casanova, Giacomo. *History of My Life: Volumes 3 & 4*. Translated by Willard R. Trask. Baltimore: Johns Hopkins University Press, 1997.

Chamberlain, Lesley. *Nietzsche in Turin: The End of the Future*. London: Quartet Books, 1996.

Connolly, Cyril. *The Unquiet Grave: A Word Cycle by Palinurus*. New York: Persea Books, 1981.

Dabhoiwala, Faramerz. "Of Sexual Irregularities, by Jeremy Bentham— Review." *Guardian*, 26 June 2014.

Davenport, Guy. *Da Vinci's Bicycle: Ten Stories*. Baltimore and London: Johns Hopkins University Press, 1979.

Descartes, René. *The Philosophical Works of Descartes*. Translated by Elizabeth S. Haldane. Cambridge: Cambridge University Press, 1911.

Gulyga, Arsenij. *Immanuel Kant: His Life and Thought*. Translated by Marijan Despalatovic. Boston: Birkhauser, 1987.

Heyerdahl, Thor. *Fatu-Hiva: Back to Nature*. New York: Doubleday, 1974.

The Illustrated Kama Sutra. Translated by Sir Richard Burton and E. F. Arbuthnot. Rochester, VT: Park Street Press, 1991.

Kang, Minsoo. "The Mechanical Daughter of Rene Descartes: The Origin and History of an Intellectual Fable." Cambridge University Press Online, 19 August 2016.

Kant, Immanuel. *Anthropology from a Pragmatic Point of View*. Translated and edited by Robert B. Louden. Cambridge: Cambridge University Press, 2006.

————. *Observations on the Feeling of the Beautiful and Sublime*. Translated by John T. Goldthwait. Berkeley and Los Angeles: University of California Press, 1984.

Kaufmann, Walter. *Nietzsche: Philosopher, Psychologist, Antichrist*. 4th ed. Princeton: Princeton University Press, 1974.

Kirk, G. S., Raven, J. E., and Schofield, M. *The Presocratic Philosophers*. 2nd ed. Cambridge: Cambridge University Press, 1983.

Mill, John Stuart, and Bentham, Jeremy. *Utilitarianism and Other Essays*. London: Penguin Books, 1987.

Monk, Ray. *Bertrand Russell: The Spirit of Solitude, 1872–1921*. New York: Free Press, 1996.

————. *Bertrand Russell: 1921–1970, The Ghost of Madness*. New York: Free Press, 2016.

————. *Ludwig Wittgenstein: The Duty of Genius*. New York: Penguin Books, 1990.

Nehring, Christina. "Heloise & Abelard: Love Hurts." *New York Times*, February 13, 2005.

Nietzsche, Friedrich. *On the Genealogy of Morals*. Translated by Walter Kaufmann. New York: Vintage Books, 1969.

————. *Thus Spoke Zarathustra*. Translated by R. J. Hollingdale. New York: Penguin Classics, 1961.

Palmer, Donald. *Does the Center Hold? An Introduction to Western Philosophy*. Mountain View, CA: Mayfield, 1991.

Rose, Phyllis. *Parallel Lives: Five Victorian Marriages*. New York: Vintage Books, 1984.

Russell, Bertrand. *A History of Western Philosophy*. New York: Simon and Schuster, 1965.

———. *Marriage and Morals*. New York: Bantam Books, 1966.

———. *The Autobiography of Bertrand Russell*. New York: Bantam Books, 1969.

Saint Augustine. *Confessions*. Translated by R. S. Pine-Coffin. New York: Penguin Books, 1961.

Scharfstein, Ben-Ami. *The Philosophers: Their Lives and the Nature of Their Thought*. New York: Oxford University Press, 1980.

Wiener, Norbert. *Cybernetics: or Control and Communication in the Animal and the Machine*. Cambridge: MIT Press, 1973.

Wittgenstein, Ludwig. *Philosophical Investigations*. Translated by G. E. M. Anscombe. New York: MacMillan, 1953.

———. *Tractatus Logico-Philosophicus*. Translated by D. F. Pears and B. F. McGuiness. London: Routledge, Kegan, and Paul, 1961.

THE IOWA SHORT FICTION AWARD AND THE
JOHN SIMMONS SHORT FICTION AWARD WINNERS,
1970–2024

Lee Abbott
Wet Places at Noon
Cara Blue Adams
You Never Get It Back
Donald Anderson
Fire Road
Dianne Benedict
Shiny Objects
A.J. Bermudez
Stories No One Hopes Are about Them
Marie-Helene Bertino
Safe as Houses
Will Boast
Power Ballads
David Borofka
Hints of His Mortality
Robert Boswell
Dancing in the Movies
Mark Brazaitis
The River of Lost Voices: Stories from Guatemala

Jack Cady
The Burning and Other Stories
Pat Carr
The Women in the Mirror
Kathryn Chetkovich
Friendly Fire
Cyrus Colter
The Beach Umbrella
Marian Crotty
What Counts as Love
Jennine Capó Crucet
How to Leave Hialeah
Jennifer S. Davis
Her Kind of Want
Janet Desaulniers
What You've Been Missing
Sharon Dilworth
The Long White
Susan M. Dodd
Old Wives' Tales
Thomas A. Dodson
No Use Pretending

Laura Valeri
The Kind of Things Saints Do
Anthony Varallo
This Day in History
Ruvanee Pietersz Vilhauer
The Water Diviner and
Other Stories
Sharon Wahl
Everything Flirts:
Philosophical Romances
Don Waters
Desert Gothic
Lex Williford
Macauley's Thumb

Miles Wilson
Line of Fall
Russell Working
Resurrectionists
Emily Wortman-Wunder
Not a Thing to Comfort You
Ashley Wurzbacher
Happy Like This
Charles Wyatt
Listening to Mozart
Don Zancanella
Western Electric